BEFORE THE DEW

A MEMOIR BY DALE LEWIS

Caprice hope you like
your book
&
Till NEXT Time !!!
SEE YA down the
Road
Dal Lew

Cover and interior design by Johnny King Design / Tulsa, OK

Published by Buffalo Dale LLC

Southwestern
STATIONERY AND BANK SUPPLY, INC.

Published in the United States of America

ISBN: 978-0-692-19000-5

FOREWARD

Located in north central New Mexico, the land where the cabin sat was remote. Miles from any neighbor it was rumored that a band of people some with little heads and arms but otherwise normal bodies once lived out in the hills nearby. Locals called them "giant midgets." This was also said to be a place where UFOs had been spotted. These sightings were usually followed by the discovery of a string of mutilated cows. The cabin was being used as a stash house by pot smugglers, and on occasion fugitives from justice had been known to stay there along with runaways and drug runners looking for work. Almost everyone was welcome except cops.

The place was just one in a network of remotely located safe houses strung across the country, each strategically located with dozens of employees. Some did business for years in legitimately run enterprises in the towns they lived in, all the while carrying on criminal activities. The entire operation was directed from Santa Fe, New Mexico, where millions of dollars were sorted and counted weekly by a few trusted men and women. Bad business deals were always settled with a gentle hand, and force was never used unless absolutely necessary. This policy was strictly followed and abuse of power was not tolerated by the boss. Drug deals gone astray resulted in boats, cars, motorcycles, even homes being repossessed and this was handled by a legal team in Albuquerque. I was there at the beginning as the pot smuggling business grew undetected from a small mom and pop business to a fleet of semis, trains, planes, and cruise ships all hauling contraband across the border.

Standing alone now on the very spot where many of the dealings took place, reflecting back 35 years it seems like I'm watching a movie about a small band of good-hearted hippies just out of high school who turned a backyard pot-selling business into a multimillion dollar operation and then lost it all. There were lots of drugs and money but for most of them it was a fast life on the way to nowhere. Now at the end of my life, it all seems to be playing out in my mind just like it was yesterday. From working for everyone from the rich and famous to big-time drug dealers to being involved in unraveling the most notorious unsolved murder in the Southwest, it's been a life of mystery, murder and love that all started in a small town in the southeast corner of Kansas.

Finding My Way

In 1951 Parsons, Kansas, a thriving railroad hub that offered any honest hard-working man a job, was where my grandfather lived and worked. Parsons also offered one of the finest hospitals in the area, which was another source of good employment, all adding up to a booming economy for the town. Although I was born there, my time in Parsons would be short as in 1953 my folks moved 120 miles south to Bartlesville, Oklahoma, where a relatively new Phillips Petroleum Company was headquartered.

Another boomtown like Parsons, Bartlesville was built on oil. In neighboring Osage County, the Osage Indians who held title to vast wealth under their ground had sold leases to men like Frank Phillips, Harry Sinclair and J. Paul Getty, all of whom drilled for oil in the area. By 1953 Phillips Petroleum Company wasn't just pulling oil out of the ground in Washington and Osage counties, they were working around the world. Phillips had just received permits to drill in many foreign countries and had obtained dozens of patents for new products including Marlex plastic at the new research laboratory located on the edge of town. Offshore drilling in the North Sea along with many other large commercial projects created lots of jobs in Bartlesville, but at the age of 3 when my folks moved there I knew nothing of that.

Frank Phillips had been dead for three years when I got to town and a young energetic Kenneth (Boots) Adams had taken his place promising to take Phillips Petroleum to even greater heights. The oil boom that was still in progress was attracting not only my family but hundreds of others looking for a better living. The early boom days had also brought bootleggers, prostitutes and a variety of thieves and killers to town, and just outside the city limits people could still find that kind of life if they were looking for it.

The first house I remember was in Ramona, a small oilfield town located between Bartlesville and Tulsa. Having an outside toilet and a 30-minute drive to Bartlesville with no heater in our old car still sticks out in my memory. Next, we moved to Bartlesville where I started school.

As a young boy growing up whenever I was on vacation from school I stayed at one or the other of my grandparents' homes. Every summer and holiday were spent either in Parsons, Kansas, where my dad's parents Ray and Zella lived, or in Pittsburg, Kansas, where my mother's parents Walter and Loretta lived on a farm. It didn't matter to me, I loved them all, and then it all fell apart. I was 8 years old when Ray died of a heart attack while working on the Katy Railroad and two years later my other grandfather Walter died. My parents would only tell me heart attacks killed them both as life took a dramatic turn. There were no more trips to Parsons or Pittsburg and both of my parents were busy working so they didn't have a lot of time to spend with me.

As a young man my father had worked as a hotel bellboy and bootlegger in Arkansas before he met my mother. I remember his first job in Bartlesville was pumping gas and changing oil at a Phillips station in town. Then after a few years he moved on to appliance repair. During this time, he developed the habit of stopping at a number of local drinking establishments before coming home which caused many arguments between my parents and often resulted in him walking out the door.

My mother also kept long hours but for different reasons. While they were still living in Parsons she had trained to be a hair stylist and nail technician. In the 1950s and 60s, unlike today, beauticians and nail specialists were all rolled into one.

Work was plentiful in her field in the oil-rich town of Bartlesville, but the pay depended on how much time she put in and with a husband whose second-grade education drew small wages there was never enough work time.

As a boy I had a slight speech impediment, making me a bit of a loner in elementary school. Although somewhat below average by school standards there were some classes I excelled in. History was one and I never missed it. The teacher was Mr. Peters and he must have been good to keep a kid like me motivated.

It was in the fifth grade I had my third encounter with death. I sat next to the smartest boy in class, George Gaede, who lived just a block down the street from my house. Every morning I would ride my bike over to George's where he stood ready and waiting with his sack lunch in hand and his bicycle pointed toward school. Riding the eight blocks we would visit about our classes or other kids and their problems. After school it was back home with us waving goodbye saying "See you later." Behind my house lay lots of pasture with some small hills dotted with trees along with a creek full of fish and plenty of wildlife. This was my playground as well as for George and several other kids in the neighborhood. From after school until we knew our folks would be looking for us this area was our fantasy land and usually it was George and me against the world. George was a good student but not particularly athletic and I was just the opposite. Around most people I was a bit shy but with George it seemed I was everyone's equal. He was the brains and I was the muscle and I defended him whenever I felt he was wronged. George had an appearance problem which some kids made fun of and I didn't like it. Average in build George's head was larger than normal for his body size. My parents told me that it was a birth defect but that meant nothing to me even after they explained it. From the day we met it didn't bother me; I liked talking to him and he liked talking to me. It was great to have such a friend but just like with my grandfathers that all ended.

It was a school day and as usual my mom had breakfast and my lunch waiting as I was off to meet my friend George then head to school. As I drew close I could see there was no George waiting. When I knocked on the door no one answered. This wasn't right. George's parents were always there in the mornings and even if he was sick, which wasn't often, they were there to tell me. I went on to school that day paying little attention to my classes, instead watching the clock thinking of George and where he might be. I rode my bike by his house after school and still no sign of George or his parents. The next morning was the same and at school the teachers would not respond to my inquiries about my friend nor would my parents. As days turned to weeks no one would talk about it. My grades which were not the best anyway got worse. I was also withdrawing more from other kids. I played with them and had friends but without George my character had changed. Throughout the year I never stopped asking about George, questioning everyone from the street crossing guard to school janitors. Six months since his disappearance I was now failing most of my classes and in desperation my folks moved to a neighboring town in hopes that new friends would help me. It would be shortly after that move on the baseball field that I solved the mystery of George's disappearance.

I had been playing little league baseball for as long as I could remember and after George's disappearance I had really gone to pushing myself, becoming one of the better players on any team I played on. In our new community baseball was big and when my skills on the field were discovered I was immediately selected for a team. It was my teammate's father, a mailman in Bartlesville where I had just moved from, who solved the mystery. During practice I began telling one of the boys about my efforts to find my missing friend and after he told me his dad was a mailman, we both thought it would be a good idea to ask for his help. At the very next practice I learned that the mail being delivered to George's house had been filling the mailbox for weeks when my new friend's dad had stopped it. There was a big container full of mail addressed to George's parents at the post office, and it was just sitting there he told me. Postal inspectors were trying to find the couple, and he had opened several letters including bills. Some were from a funeral home looking for payment for the burial of a boy named George he said. What had happened to my friend or the whereabouts of his parents I didn't know. Strangely as the news soaked in I felt relief. In my mind, George my friend was back and I could see his face again, something I realized I hadn't been able to do for a long while. As time went on my grades improved but looking back I can see I kept a distance from most people for the fear death could happen again. I did become close with a boy named Mike Davis who lived next door but three years later he moved away and I felt deserted once more.

BEFORE THE DEW

A Youth in America

1960s America was in the midst of enormous change. A new generation was bringing new thoughts to the way American kids saw things, and I was right in the middle of it all. Although my high school grades were getting a bit better I sure wasn't a scholar, just average at best. One thing I did have going for me was a desire to please my high school coaches. Any sport, all a coach had to do was ask me to try out and that was it. I was always willing, excelling in some sports and average in others but a little school like Dewey, Oklahoma, often just needed bodies to back up real athletes and in the late 1960s that's what I did.

In small schools coaches are also teachers and having coaches as my instructors would turn out to be a tremendous help in getting my high school diploma. I found some of the guys playing sports could barely read or write so a kid like me with Cs and Ds must have looked brilliant. Upon graduating high school, I was a bit lost when I was thrown out into the world but I did know one thing, it was 1970 and the war in Vietnam was in full swing. With little direction in life and not much education I was just the kind of kid the draft boards wanted, so college started looking like a better way for me to go. I had two problems and one was money. My folks could help me some and I had a little saved but I'd have to borrow the rest and that was just for the first year. My other problem was time. I had but a few months at best before the draft board would be looking for me and I needed a plan.

Beginning in the ninth grade between sports and school, I'd worked at a fancy high-end restaurant in Bartlesville called The Embers. I started off as a dishwasher and over the years

I worked my way up to busboy and part-time cook. Always in need of extra money, I also came in after closing and cleaned the place up.

Through the years I got several of my neighborhood buddies' jobs there, and over time I became so valuable to the owners that in order to save them having to come down to the restaurant all the time they gave me the keys to the place. It was a great job for a kid and I took full advantage of it. Now at age 18 I was either going to college or into the armed services, so I'd have to give it up. I was at loose ends and when my buddy Jim Roberds got a summer job at Rabbit Ears Lodge in Colorado it looked like a good place for me to go and try to get my thoughts together. The Lodge was owned by Phillips Petroleum Company and they catered to their employees who loved the outdoors. Jim had called me saying there was a job available and money to be made if I wanted to come up, so with little thought I just decided to go. I wasn't at all prepared to leave town for the summer but it all sounded good to me except I didn't have a car. The small motorcycle I used to get around town wasn't something that was going to make the 700-mile drive to the lodge. In our conversation Jim had told me the job was waiting, but I needed to hurry so the next day with a small bag in hand I got a ride to the edge of town and stuck out my thumb.

Living near US-75 which is a major highway I had often seen hitchhikers. It looked easy and my first ride came quickly but after two days on the road I wasn't even close to my destination. I brought a sleeping bag and a few clothes, a roll of toilet paper and a toothbrush so I wasn't desperate for anything but a shower and transportation. Finally, on my third day out I was able to catch a ride with a big rig trucker who would be passing close to the exit in Colorado that led to the lodge. During the six hour-drive I learned his name was Frank and he was headed to San Francisco with an express delivery from the East Coast that was way overdue. We passed the time visiting about where he lived and our general likes and dislikes and as we got close to my exit he made me an offer. He still had another 36 hours of straight driving time in front of him and having someone to talk to would help him stay awake. If I would agree to make the rest of the trip with him he'd pay me and buy me a bus ticket back to Colorado or home to Bartlesville. I didn't have much time to make up my mind one way or another, he needed to keep this rig moving, and sitting in that comfortable seat was sure better than sitting out on the highway. As we passed the exit for Rabbit Ears Lodge Frank said it would be all right to take a nap if I wanted because he'd need me more in a couple of hours so that's what I did. The passenger seat in his semi was quite nice and laid way back and with the rumble of the motor in the background I was dead to the world in no time.

Around three hours later I awoke to the sound of Frank's voice telling me he was getting tired and asking if I would get some water and a washcloth out of his bag so he could wash his face. It was obvious this guy hadn't planned on stopping until he got to San Francisco no matter what and now I was along for the ride. Climbing over the seat I grabbed his bag and opened it. There were several bottles of water, some sandwiches, a couple of prescription pill bottles, and an assortment of candy bars along with a washcloth that I poured some water on and handed to him. That's all he needed and another few hours would pass before we stopped for a much-needed bathroom break with Frank telling me in advance to be quick and if I didn't hurry back to the truck he'd leave me. I'd been riding with him for 16 hours and had another 20 to go. We had mostly run out of things to talk about and now it was up to the little white pills in those pill bottles to keep him awake.

He called it speed and said he'd been taking them for years with no bad side effects nonetheless, when he offered some I refused. That three-hour nap would be the last I saw in a hair-raising ride that ended when he let me out on the outskirts of San Francisco. I had seen his good side when he handed a $20 bill to a homeless man when we took a bathroom break, but I had also seen his bad side when after a motorist cut him off he acted like he would ram his car. With his diesel roaring up the great mountains of the Continental Divide and then down the mountains at break neck speed, I felt lucky to be alive.

Either luck or God was on my side because I'd barely gotten my bedroll out of his truck when a Volkswagen van stopped and the driver asked if I needed a ride. A hippie -looking dude who was around 25, he had long blonde hair that reached halfway down his back and said his name was Alex. Sitting next to him was a slim girl with shoulder-length dark hair who looked about the same age. She was just as friendly and was introduced as Sue. He just said "get in" and I did. Driving down the road I told them my story about my friend Jim and Rabbit Ears Lodge, the truck ride and Frank, then without my even asking, the two offered me a place to stay for the night. Apparently, I must have looked like I could use a little cleaning up and some much-needed sleep.

Back in Dewey I'd heard about flower power and the free love movement that was going on in San Francisco and now here I was in the heart of it. Things could not have worked out better for me and as it turned out their apartment was one block away from the famous Haight-Asbury district where the hippie movement had all started. As soon as we arrived they showed me the shower and told me where to sleep saying they would see me after I got some rest. Closing my eyes, it felt a bit strange to me. I'd never felt so much kindness and concern from perfect strangers. After 10 hours of sleep I felt like a new man and over some food I started to learn more about my new friends.

Alex was originally from Texas and was one of a group of men working on remodeling a building that sat just a couple bus stops away. The job consisted of stripping old paint off of walls at an apartment complex and they were always needing help. Without a lot of money in my pocket and a long way from Rabbit Ears Lodge, the job felt perfect to me. I would be paid daily meaning that in a few days if I liked it out here in San Francisco I would be able to rent my own place for the rest of the summer, and if I didn't I'd just get a bus ticket home. Alex and Sue were fine with that and a few days later Sue helped me find a one-room pay-by-the-week apartment. It wasn't fancy and I shared a bath but it was furnished and cheap. With steady work I was also pocketing a little cash every week.

When I wasn't busy working I was sightseeing with Sue who was always up for showing me a new part of town. Turned out she was from the area and knew all the hot spots for music. Alex played a pretty mean guitar and over the next couple of months the two of them took me to music clubs and festivals, introducing me to everything that was happening in this new age. The peace and love stuff hadn't hit Oklahoma yet but if Alex and Sue were a part of it I wanted to be too.

The summer ended quickly for me and it happened when all of us were celebrating Alex's birthday. Sue had brought a cake for lunch to the worksite and a small group of friends and fellow workers had gathered. While she was slicing the cake one of the older guys whom none of us really knew made a remark about Sue's figure and from where I was standing it looked like he touched her. That's all it took for me and after demanding he apologize before long I made sure he regretted his action. Even though I'd been enlightened by the peace movement I wouldn't stand for something like that after all they'd done for me but now I was out of a job. I told Alex and Sue it was time for me to get back to Oklahoma anyway, and with a kiss on my cheek from Sue and a handshake from Alex we parted. Just like in death I knew we would never see each other again and I didn't like it.

The trip home was long but fairly uneventful. With money in my pocket I had decided to take a bus back which gave me plenty of time to think. Arriving home, I learned several older boys I knew from school had just been killed in Vietnam and with the TV and radio all talking about the protests going on about the war I was as nervous as ever about the draft. I started thinking that maybe I could make a junior college basketball team and even get a scholarship. It was a wild thought but in high school basketball had been my sport. I played and lettered in football, track, and baseball but basketball was my game. Not fast or particularly quick my hand-eye coordination was excellent. In high school and now playing some pickup games I made passes that dazzled all my coaches and at times I could as they say shoot the lights out. With a deferral from the draft board to go to college and hopes of a basketball career, a small junior college in Miami, Oklahoma, would become my next home.

I had four friends from high school who lived near me. Jim Roberds, Dan Shoup, Rob Schmidt, and another was Don Irwin who was planning to attend college in Miami and had offered to share a dorm room. A good student he would become a stable force in my life, tutoring me with my homework, even consoling my ego when I got cut from the basketball team. Making the team had been a long shot at best but Don helped me with my classes and kept me in school. Like many college kids I was always worried about money. Although my parents helped me out some and I had a part-time job as a doorman at a nightclub outside town funds were always short.

With my first year coming to an end I needed to find a good-paying job for the upcoming summer. At a college job fair, I found it working with the Green Giant Company in Belvidere, Illinois, picking peas and corn. This was a summer job that guaranteed lots of money and the company was recruiting college kids in dozens of states to do all kinds of work. To make things even better, the recruiter told me my job would start as soon as I could get there.

On my last day of school with clothes already packed I was more than ready to get out of Miami. After a stop in Dewey for a couple of days with a full tank of gas in the old car I was driving, I headed north. It would take me a day and a half to drive there, and when I got to Belvidere I found 600 other college kids from all over the country living in bunkhouses on a large compound that was just outside of town. After checking in I was put on a crew of about 50 others and assigned to a bunkhouse then given the lowdown on where to eat my meals and told to be prepared to work the next day. I spent the first couple days along with everyone else learning how to operate their equipment. The bosses told us then that the work would be nonstop after training and it was.

We worked 12-to-15 hour a day shifts and more if we could take it, seven days a week. When the peas and corn were ready for harvest we worked, picking thousands of acres for as far as the eye could see in some fields. I liked it and I also had a bit of an advantage because of my experience spending summers helping on my grandpa's farm as a boy. Grandpa had lots of cows and did some farming and usually when I came for the summer I helped with all that along with hauling hay to the barn. I always liked this summer farm work so I was a natural fit for the Green Giant people and soon made assistant foreman. I also had another advantage which was the ability to read people as far as who was good and bad and who wanted to work and who just acted like they did. This was a gift I had since childhood.

I didn't know any of these guys but it didn't take long to figure out who I could depend on and who I couldn't. It didn't really matter to me, I worked anyway and the ones who wanted to make money got up and worked with me. Taking into consideration that most of the group we had were city kids it was a pretty good crew. Except for going to college, a lot of these guys had never been away from home let alone driven a huge tractor pulling a two-story harvester. A full-time tractor repair shop and the nurse's station were always busy and just three weeks into the job I found myself along with one of my crew in for an unexpected visit to the nurse.

Peas grow on vines which for harvesting are cut into rows similar to the way hay is cut before a hay baler machine comes along picking up the rows of cut hay then throwing bales of hay out the back end. A pea combine will pick up the rows of cut vines then tumble the vines around in a barrel-type contraption similar in size to a concrete truck spinning the vines around inside that separate the peas from the vine. The combine then throws the vines out the back end after the peas have been separated. The peas are put into a big tub that sits atop the harvester. When it's full, a semi-truck pulls up beside it and the harvester dumps the tub into the semi's trailer which is then hauled back to the plant. These big spinning hoppers that separate the peas from the vines often get plugged up with the vines if you drive your tractor too fast in the vine picking-up process. When that happens the only thing to do is to climb inside the back end of the hopper and throw the vines out by hand until you can clear the congestion. I knew this because it had happened to me. It's extremely hot inside the drums and cleaning them out is a tricky thing to do even for experienced farm kids.

Doug who I got to know pretty well while playing some pickup basketball at the company's outdoor court was one of the guys who always wanted to work. Any time there was work he showed up. It was during one of those long hot days that Doug got himself into trouble. The cutting crew had already done their job cutting the peas earlier in the day and now the peas were all laying in a long line. We always traveled in caravans usually 10 to 12 rigs in a row and pulling off the road into the field, Doug was the lead tractor. He was going a little faster than he should have been and his harvester got plugged up pretty quickly. As I slowly passed him on my tractor I could see he was already off his and heading toward the back end of the harvester where he would have to climb in to hand toss the pea vines out that small trap door. The field we were in was another one of those big ones. A circle down and back to the front where we started could take a good hour, maybe more. As I reached the end of the field and turned heading back down another row, the other tractors were all close by but Doug's was still where he had stopped to clean out his rig. I thought it a bit unusual to be taking so long and as I got closer he was nowhere to be seen. The ground behind his unit which should have had a large pile of pea vines behind it was bare. He couldn't have gone anywhere, I could see in every direction, and then it hit me. Doug was in that hopper. Shutting down my tractor I ran to the back of his and started hollering for him. Climbing up and looking through the trap door I saw Doug lying in the hopper unconscious. When I hollered his name, there was no response, then waving at the other drivers I climbed in. Fresh cut pea vines create their own kind of heat and with a ton of fresh cut vines all around it became apparent I had to act quickly. I didn't know what had happened to him but grabbing the back collar of his shirt I dragged him toward the small trap door. My face and clothes were already covered in sweat and the sunlight from the door was the only light coming into the dark drum. As I pushed Doug out through the hole we both fell the 10 feet to the ground. It was a soft landing and I was okay as the other boys surrounding me were offering water and putting wet rags around my neck. Doug was still out and we were all worried but when the field foreman got there he started coming around. We both went to the nurse's station, and when I returned to the bunkhouse that night after being checked out I found I had become a bit of a hero for my quick action in getting Doug out. The crew had spread the word about what I had done and the next day a company spokesman presented me with a small check as a bonus for helping to promote safety. I was doing pretty well in Belvidere and with basketball games always going on I liked living on the five-acre compound.

Besides all the college-aged kids, there were another hundred or so seasonal workers staying there. These guys were older fellows some of whom I felt were a bit shady and there was one man on my crew who I couldn't avoid despite my misgivings about him.

Even though he was missing one arm, I knew Sam was a dangerous man from the day I met him. I heard he'd lost his arm while working on a tractor at the Giant several years earlier. He'd received a settlement but locals told me he'd spent all that cash on hard whiskey and gambling and now he was broke and doing whatever work the company would give him in order to have some cash and a bed in the bunkhouse. It also meant he had to live with a lot of noisy college kids which I figured would eventually lead to trouble. Then on top of it all I ended up being his boss which I didn't like and was sure he didn't either. Rumored to have been a good mechanic at one time in his life, now he was driving a tractor pulling a harvester which I could see was a bit degrading to him. It all added up to a 50-year-old hard-ass with a bad attitude for any kid that crossed him at the wrong time, and I just knew before the season was over something bad was going to happen.

The summer had been unusually hot but the harvest was going well. We were the top crew out of 16 and bonuses were given every two weeks at payday, so everyone was tired but happy. It never failed that somewhere in the compound a poker game would be going on after payday mostly among people between shift changes or kids who just didn't go to work. With no security guards in the barracks to keep strangers out at times there were even people playing that no one knew.

Liquor flowed freely at these games along with marijuana but it didn't bother me. Many of my friends back home drank and were smoking weed now so I just let it pass by. My time was spent either at work or on a basketball court with a company team which 10 of us had formed. Playing in both a church league and with the company team when I could turned out to be a lot of fun. There were three guys from Knoxville, Tennessee, two from Nebraska, a Texas kid, a couple others from Oklahoma, myself and a straggler or two from the bunkhouse so we always had enough for a game. Like me most of the other fellows had played a little college ball somewhere along the way and together we were pretty good.

Time went by fast. It had been a great summer and with the harvest season getting near the end I wasn't looking forward to saying goodbye to my basketball buddies. As usual I had come back to the compound late and walking through the canteen area I could see a card game going on in another of the bunkhouses nearby. Old one-armed Sam, two college kids and another man about Sam's age were all engaged in a big game. After showering and passing through the area again I noticed the boys had apparently decided after losing all their money that either Sam or the other fellow had been cheating and heated words were being exchanged. I'd heard Sam was handy with a knife and not afraid to use it and one of the boys worked for me. This kid was a bit green around the ears but I liked him and was afraid he was getting himself into something where he might get hurt.

Sam and I had never had any trouble but it was still a risky move as I immediately interrupted telling all of them that the game was over and if they wanted a job to hit the sack. I said it in a stern tone meant to intimidate. Although I was 6 feet 2 inches tall and a tight 220 pounds it was all a bluff on my part. I wasn't a bad-ass and looking at Sam I felt he knew it. He wasn't the type of guy to lay his cards right out in front of anyone but my bluff worked on the boys and as far as I knew that night the game ended. At sunup the next morning it was work as usual with one exception, there was no Sam to be found. I reported his absence to my main lead man as soon as he arrived, and we both thought it was strange when we found out his car and belongings were all gone too. It didn't mean much to me except he was a good hand who usually came to work every day, drunk or sober. That night when I arrived back at the compound I was told the cops had been looking for me and that a man's body had been found just outside the compound gate.

I didn't even have time to shower or absorb the news before Green Giant management and the cops were questioning my involvement in the card game and the ruckus the night before. The body turned out to be the older guy who had been playing cards with Sam and the boys. He had been stabbed several times and sliced open across the gut the cops told me. Apparently, he bled to death in the tall grass just outside the gate. The other two boys had told them that I had broken up the card game and that I was some kind of tough guy myself. After an hour of questioning by the cops my version of the events the night before must have been the same as that of the two other boys. The cops weren't after me at all. They knew who one-armed Sam was and were looking for him. It didn't surprise them that he'd cut up somebody, he'd done it before, but a killing on Green Giant property with a lot of missing money was going to make the newspapers. Company officials also asked me to retell the story several times in their offices before they were satisfied I had nothing to do with the murder. Meanwhile the two boys were telling everyone at the compound I had saved them from a knife- wielding card shark. Just like Doug and the combine incident, the story of the card game was taking on a life of its own and once again I was rewarded by the Green Giant Company for how I handled myself.

With a bonus in my pocket and a new job title as field boss

I was feeling pretty good. The summer wrapped up a few weeks later and after promising to return next season with some good Oklahoma farm boys it looked like I might just be in line for a real company job. I knew the other two boys and I would have to be witnesses against Sam if the police ever caught him but I wasn't worried. Rumor had it that he moved to the fertile California coast where he had been harvesting avocados until he cut up a couple of Mexican farm workers. From my time spent in California I knew many migrant workers lived in the state and with no IDs required it would make sense for a man on the run to be there. One thing I was sure of, with the cops looking for him Sam wouldn't be around Belvidere the next summer.

When I returned to Oklahoma for fall classes it didn't take long to see I wasn't going to make it through another year of school. Don was doing great but for me if a subject wasn't interesting and I missed a few classes there was no way I could get caught up, so I quit going to that class. Before long I was missing classes that I liked, too. The only thing I was doing was playing intramural basketball, and when the school cancelled my college ID that ended too. Still living with Don in the dorm room I got through the rest of the year working security at a bar, all the while making a list of guys who wanted to make some money working for the Green Giant Company in the upcoming summer.

While recruiting fellows to work, I happened to hear about jobs working on cattle and sheep ranches outside Deadwood, South Dakota. The kid I got the information from wasn't looking for a job, he was a college student in Miami. He came from the Deadwood area and during a pick-up basketball game he told me about all the ranch work available in his home state. I was killing time waiting for the summer harvest season to start so I just figured why not check it out. If I got a job it would be good, and if not, at least I was seeing a new area of the country.

The kid was right, after a two -day drive about 50 miles

outside Deadwood at a small-town grocery store a rancher struck up a conversation after seeing the Oklahoma tags on my car. He ended up offering me a job on his ranch and a place to stay and I started the next day. Our agreement was simple. He'd pay me daily or weekly, whichever I wanted, give me a place to live and feed me. In return I'd give him a few days' notice when I had to leave for Belvidere to start working for the Green Giant. From sunup to sundown I fed cows and helped him deliver calves. He had sheep too, hundreds of them, but their maintenance was far less than the cows. It was calving season and it seemed there was always trouble with the cows. One of my many responsibilities was to help him look for mama cows about to have their babies and if possible try to keep track of them. The rancher was most afraid of mountain lions and wolves. A baby calf had little hope if one of these predators got its smell. They could also be dangerous to men, and I found that out when late one night a mountain lion actually jumped up on the hood of my truck. But overall for the two months I had the time of my life driving the beautiful, remote hills of South Dakota.

I arrived at the Green Giant compound a bit earlier than the rest of the boys I'd recruited so I could welcome them. The peas and corn had been getting a lot of rain so I anticipated another money-making summer ahead. The boys that Green Giant had hired also started drifting into camp and the company put me to work training them all. I was one of a couple dozen instructors training the boys on the equipment. Some kids just weren't cut out to operate something like these huge tractors and harvesters that were 60 feet long and so tall and heavy that when traveling down roads we sometimes had to avoid bridges. The boys who we felt couldn't handle these rigs were assigned to other jobs.

My guys were all thrown into a pool with the 600 others and by the time it was all over I was left with four of my original 20 recruits. A few days later I got the call that one of the pea fields about 50 miles away had been tested and the peas were ripe and ready for harvest.

I soon discovered that this year would be different from my first one. The real trouble started the first week when another crew boss told me two of the fellows I'd brought from Oklahoma had sideswiped their tractors, causing a harvester to flip over onto its side. The drivers were okay but the harvester was heavily damaged, and unless I wanted the two on my crew, he was going to fire them. I found the two boys back at the bunkhouse later drinking beer and laughing about their mishaps that day. I didn't see the humor in it I told them; they could have been killed. But my comment went unnoticed. These guys just didn't care. Luckily for us all, the next day the two were gone. Then another one of my so-called "recommended men" was arrested on outstanding warrants and two more got into a fight with some locals. The harvesting season had just begun and already there were fewer than half left of the guys I had hired from Oklahoma, which I was sure didn't look good for me up at Green Giant headquarters.

I knew the other field foremen weren't happy with me, and I was having my own crew problems by this time. First, a refueling truck driver let the diesel fuel overflow and the tractor caught on fire. No one was hurt but the tractor sustained heavy damage. The driver, who was a local kid, had been so worried about what would happen to him that he left the scene. Despite the fire extinguishers that were on every tractor he took off and let it burn. I wanted to fire him so badly I couldn't see straight, but I couldn't find the kid anywhere. A few weeks later some cars at the bunkhouse were broken into, and it looked like a couple of my guys had been involved in that, too. As incident after incident happened, my career with Green Giant went down the tubes. Some of the fellows from Oklahoma quit and headed home; others found factory jobs in town and rented apartments. It wasn't just my crew, I'd seen the same thing happen the year before. Out of about 600 initial recruits, a fourth left within the first month. Then crews would be combined, which was about to happen to my crew. I was frustrated but I kept working, taking a job with another crew. I was back to driving a tractor 12 to 16 hours a day, which by now was okay with me. I was making money without the headaches and disappointments of being a supervisor. Before long I was socializing and drinking with some of the guys who had quit and going to the wild parties they held at their apartment in town. My hopes for a company job were dashed when a half-smoked joint was found in a Green Giant car I had been driving. Although the joint wasn't mine, I had no way to prove it because the supervisors shared all the cars. I was eventually found innocent but by then I had quit my job and gone to work in one of the local factories putting electric fans together.

I moved into a two-bedroom apartment occupied by eight guys and sometimes just as many women with loud music, drinking and parties all night. I knew it wasn't going to last long. Out of all the Okies I had recruited three guys were left in the apartment plus another two from Tennessee, one from Florida, and a couple that no one knew where they called home.

Lots of Tennessee fellows still worked for Green Giant and since our door was never locked many of them stopped by regularly, usually bringing other friends. In general, we all got along. Some, like me, were involved with sports while others had their own pursuits but most of us liked going to bars with live music. More often than not someone would get lucky and pick up a girl and that girl would have friends, and the party would be on. Either because of my size and good physical condition or because I still felt like the boss, I wound up being a sort of marshal over this group trying to keep things from getting out of control.

The three remaining Oklahoma guys were about to head back

to college and with my career with the Giant finished, I was thinking about school again myself. Although I hadn't made as much money as I had planned, I had made some new friends, who like Alex and Sue a few years earlier, had opened my eyes to a bigger world. I still adhered to the Christian principles I had been raised with about how to live and to treat people as you would want to be treated, but I had learned there was another side to life.

The party house ended when Edward, a local guy I didn't really like, was forcing himself onto an unwilling girl in a back bedroom. The fight started quickly with me throwing the first punch. I don't think anyone but the creep Edward really knew what started it, but the fight turned into an all-out brawl, tearing up the apartment and continuing out into the yard. It seemed like it was over as fast as it started with all of us knowing the cops would be there soon. I hurriedly grabbed my one suitcase, got into my truck, and down the road I went. The other Oklahomans followed my lead and for the next few days the three of us stayed at a campground outside town.

The summer was over and with little reason to hang around we all decided to head back to Miami but I wasn't there long. College didn't seem the right fit for me and I missed the enrollment deadline. I moved back home and without any sense of direction, for about six months the only constructive thing I did was play basketball at the Bartlesville YMCA. I was playing in the noon hour men's business league, the evening men's league, an industrial league, and I coached grade school kids after school and then refereed their games on Saturday mornings.

Toward the end of the YMCA basketball season wondering what my next move should be, a new opportunity caught my attention. Some older guys I had previously worked construction with told me a guy could make a lot of money in Tucson, Arizona, and it sounded interesting. They said a lot of construction work was going on down there and without any winter weather I could stay busy year-round. Rent was cheap they said and a couple of colleges were in town if I wanted to try school again along with a nice YMCA for basketball. I was sold from the get go so with a couple of phone numbers in hand of some hometown people I heard lived there and a little cash in my pocket, I headed for Tucson.

Bordertown Arizona

I knew nothing about the town of Tucson except it was going to be a three-day drive from Bartlesville and all I had was a few clothes, an old pick-up, my small savings and those phone numbers. I didn't know what his reaction would be after all these years but I planned to call Billy Trent first. I remembered that we had been pretty good friends in grade school because like me he was athletic but also a little shy. His parents still lived in the same house, and when I stopped by before leaving town, they were thrilled to see me and happy to give me his phone number. Even if he couldn't help me I thought it would be great to catch up with my old friend.

As soon as I got to town I found a cheap hotel room and took a few days to get my bearings, then I called Billy. He was glad to hear from me and immediately told me about a room I could rent from some friends of his who frequently traveled for long periods of time. I'd be sharing a house with three others and he warned me upfront that they got high. If pot smoking bothered me he said this wouldn't work out.

By the late 1970s most people I knew had smoked pot. It was a craze just hitting the middle of the country, and even the rednecks were starting to get high. My two summers at Green Giant had exposed me to more pot smokers, as half the camp got loaded on more than alcohol. For me though working out seemed to do the trick. I would drink but the pot smoking, not that much. I had never even smoked a cigarette, but it was the fad going around.

I told him I was cool with it and two hours later I was checking out a very nice two-story adobe home. It was definitely better than the motel and I jumped on it without even meeting my new roommates who Billy said were out of town for a couple of weeks. Billy also thought he could help me out when I told him I was going to start looking for work. He introduced me to Chuck Biscuit, the owner of a roofing company, who immediately gave me a job. It was a darn good thing I was in shape as the first few days just about did me in. This was hard manual labor working alongside mostly Mexican men who had done this kind of work in this kind of climate their whole lives. In the beginning my legs and hands cramped up so badly that I missed a day here or there or sometimes took off early. The Mexicans laughed at my weakness behind my back in Spanish which kind of pissed me off at first but in a couple of weeks I could stay up with the best of them. The work was hard but the pay was good and I grew to like my co-workers.

As Billy and I were getting reacquainted it turned out that he had other friends from Oklahoma living in Tucson who he thought I might enjoy meeting. Now in my late 20s I still adhered to what I'd been taught in church about the dangers of hanging out with the wrong kind of folks. I'd seen in the past the trouble bad people can cause but the new people Billy was talking about sounded like pretty good folks.

My first encounter with these new friends of Billy's took place at a huge concert with several major acts held in an 18,000-seat horseshoe-shaped pavilion. Billy and my boss from the roofing company had gotten an extra ticket and offered it to me. We all met up at the home of another one of the Oklahoma guys Billy wanted me to meet for a pre-party that was underway when I arrived. He lived in a beautiful house that made mine look like a dump by comparison and a couple dozen people all decked out in fancy clothing were already there having a good time. Not really knowing anyone, at first, I felt out of place but the friendliness of the group soon put me at ease. After Billy introduced me around a bit, I met Jonah, the homeowner. While visiting about Oklahoma and the work I'd been doing in

Arizona he said he'd like to talk with me further and asked me to call him. It sounded like he might have some work for me so I gladly took his number.

At the concert I sat with several people from the party, on the side to the left of the stage, about 50 rows up. Another group I'd met from the house, including Billy and Jonah, had front-row seats. This was quite a deal for me, just an average working guy getting to hang out with some obviously very wealthy people. It hadn't been that long ago that I'd been driving that tractor for the Green Giant. Before the show started beach balls and Frisbees started flying everywhere. It was one big party with about 18,000 people. My new group of friends was also passing around something I'd already heard of called magic mushroom, and joints were handed out like candy. I passed on the mushrooms but the pot smoke was so thick I got high just from being there. In the middle of all this wild fun I caught a Frisbee and not knowing anyone but the people in our group on the front row, I took aim their way. It was a long shot just to make it that far, so I stood up, and adjusting for distance and arch, I threw it as hard as I could. Three girls who were sitting beside me started hollering and clapping but as the Frisbee got closer it went to the right and hit an unsuspecting target. It was a fellow I'd seen at the party, a large man of around 300 pounds with red hair. He had been a tad unfriendly but I hadn't noticed he was with the others on the front row until the Frisbee hit him. The guy had been looking in another direction when the Frisbee smacked him full force against the back of his head and I knew it had to hurt. I was still standing on my seat and everyone else in my group was laughing as he immediately turned and somehow with all the people around looked right at me with a look I didn't like at all. It was an innocent mistake. Hundreds of people were throwing things around and as the music started I tried to forget it. The concert was great and my new female friends who told me they'd just gotten back into town from a month-long business trip also turned out to be my roommates.

As time went on and I gained their trust, I learned that Billy's friends who I was now sharing a house with were into the marijuana smuggling business big time. It wasn't long after Billy told me he was looking for a trustworthy person in good shape for some kind of upcoming pot deal and thought I might like the extra money. Apparently, Billy and his friends had wanted to feel me out before they trusted me with any information about their business. I must have passed their test because he said if I wanted in I could start with the next shipment.

It wasn't a big load, just a half dozen Mexicans, or mules, as Billy called them, carrying as much weight as they could in the darkness of night on a 12-mile walk over the border near the Mexican town of Nogales where another man would have a car waiting to pick me and the load up.

Billy told me they always sent one of their own people with the mules to make sure the delivery got dropped off at the right location. The pay was very good and if I wanted I could carry some product myself and make some extra cash. That roofing job was getting hotter and hotter, and the money I could make in one night added up to a month of my roofing pay. It didn't take me long to make up my mind and three days later I was dropped off at the U.S.-Mexican border check station. Dressed in all black, wearing a good pair of hiking shoes, carrying a canteen and a pocketful of money, I thought the Mexican cops had to know what I was doing.

Before I got out of the car, Billy said that since this was my first time, a trusted runner who spoke a little English would be my guide, and he told me to make sure to give him extra money. He also said that the police could be in the area of the pickup so I might have to wait awhile depending on those Mexican cops.

I was dumb, but I was tempted by the lifestyle I'd seen with parties, money and women. Now I was over the border with the address of a man named Pasqual, and the taxi driver who picked me up knew exactly where I was going before I said a word. When we got to his house Pasqual met me at the door. He was a friendly acting fellow who spoke broken English and seemed to understand me well. Billy had said they did a lot of business with him and there would be no trouble, just give him the pre-counted money and follow his instructions. That was exactly what I planned to do. Pasqual's adobe house was probably one of the better homes in Nogales. The inside was full of nice furniture with a big Harley-Davidson motorcycle right in the middle. We sat at a table full of jewelry and money, lots of money. When I handed him my cash without even counting it he just added it to the pile. The Mexican runners were already there along with my guide who Pasqual introduced me to. All were dressed like me in black, carrying canteens. These men would be my companions for the 12-mile walk. They would drop the shipment off and walk the 12 miles back all in one night. By now it was getting dark. I was ready, and after a few more instructions from Pasqual and a few in Spanish to the Mexican runners, a truck pulled around. We all loaded up, each carrying a gunny sack and down a back road we went, leaving Pasqual behind with a big grin, waving goodbye.

There was no turning back and soon we were outside of town. Without much being said we were dropped off in the desert and the march began. It was probably a good thing that Billy hadn't told me a lot about the trek except it would be tough. In order for the Mexicans to get back before daylight, they had to move, and move they did. After a couple of hours when I asked for a break I found out from my guide they didn't care if I followed them or not. They had already been paid for the job, and he said it would be best if I kept up. The guide showed very little sympathy, and I started thinking what a bad idea this had been. I couldn't understand a word they were saying but knew if I stopped, they would leave me. We did stop occasionally when the lead runner gave a hand signal to halt so he could listen for sounds. Mexican cops ahead, the guide told me on one of these stops. Like a fool, to make some extra money I was packing a gunny sack of weed and lying there for what seemed to be an hour. I told myself if I get out of this I'm going home to Oklahoma and never coming back. You couldn't see a thing on this moonless night, but I could sure hear those cops. They were really close but we all held our place until the sound of those footsteps drifted off. I was sure the Mexicans had been through this before and were only concerned for their own safety. If we were discovered these guys would just drop their load and head for home on a run. But me, with a wad of cash in my pocket that I had to pay to the guide and all this pot, either way out in the middle of nowhere I was probably a dead man. I was praying to God like I'd never done before as the voices faded and the march started back up. Like thc lying fool I was, I kept hold of that gunny sack thinking surely, we were close to our destination, but we kept going. I was also keeping my eye on a snowy mountain top the guide was occasionally pointing out to me. It was his reference point, and I knew it was important in case these guys decided to bolt on me, which I was beginning to think could happen any time.

We were either going up or coming down small hills full of loose rocks in the full dead of night, and I started thinking about snakes, which are common in southern Arizona. What a fool I was to be wearing ordinary hiking shoes that were only ankle high. I was a fool over and over I kept telling myself, trying to follow in the same steps as the fellow in front of me. Slipping on the downside of a hill I often got behind them and whenever I did I had to stop for a second and listen for their footsteps ahead of me so I could catch up. Then the inevitable happened. On one of these occasions after taking a little time to catch my breath, there was no sound when I stood up. Taking a drink from my now half-empty canteen I realized I was all alone and my only thought was to head for that snowy mountain peak that damn guide had told me to follow if I got lost. It didn't seem like I'd gone far when I heard a frightening rattle. I dropped my bag and jumped like I'd never jumped before, took a couple steps, and froze. The rattle had stopped and I could see my gunny sack maybe 15 feet away. I hadn't noticed before but in the moonlight it had a different brownish color to it and it wasn't that far away. I was preoccupied with being lost and thinking about retrieving that gunny sack where a deadly snake might be curled up waiting when a tap on my shoulder made me jump again.

It was my guide. He had heard the noise and not being far away had come back. Speaking softly, he said the rest of the guys were just over the hill and to fetch my bag and come on. I had no time to think and I knew he wouldn't come back for me again. The trip had already been delayed by those cops, and I was starting to see I was dragging them down as well. Three big steps backward and in a flash, I had that bag in my hand. We marched on and my gut feeling was that we had to be close to our destination. As we came to a group of large trees from a distance there appeared to be someone hanging by his arms in one of them.

When I got closer it became clear that it was a person in the tree, and I stopped briefly but a tap on my shoulder meant "Come on." After maybe another half mile the leader lowered his bag and the others followed. I thanked God, then reached into my pocket and pulled out the money I had been told to give to the guide. The trip wasn't over for me yet, but after all I'd been through I felt relieved to have made it to the pickup spot. I'd also brought a little extra cash with me, and as I shook the guide's hand in gratitude, I dug deep into my pocket, giving him all I had. Without a word they all disappeared into the night, and all of a sudden, I was alone. I wondered had they walked me past that body in the tree as a warning that this could happen to me?

After a couple of hours of waiting and thinking, the sun came up and I could finally see my surroundings. From where I was hiding in some small brush I could see a road straight ahead. I could have kissed that Mexican guide right on the lips. But now I realized my scheduled pickup time was around noon and I was already out of water. With the blistering sun coming up fast my situation soon became serious. Dehydrated from the night before, my legs and fingers were cramping up. I noticed a lone cattle trough not too far away and started thinking it might contain water. Would the water be drinkable I kept asking myself? Billy had warned me not to wear any jewelry so I didn't have a watch. As time went on, by looking at the sun I felt noon had come and gone and still no pickup man. It had to be 110 degrees in the shade what there was of it. There hadn't been a single car on the road and I was sure I could get to that water trough and back before anyone would see me. Getting desperate, I decided to try it.

I was about halfway there when out of nowhere I saw a car approaching fast or was it a truck? The sun had practically blinded me. Turning to run back to my hiding spot I lost my sense of where I had come from and fell into a ditch. What if these guys were bandits or worse? I told myself to lay there and be quiet, then I heard someone yelling, "Get in!" Even if it was the cops I didn't care. They had to have water and I needed water badly. I heard people scrambling around throwing stuff into the car that was now right beside me, but I still didn't know who they were, pickup guys or cops. When I got in the car they gave me some water, and drinking slowly, I started coming back to life. We were almost back to Santa Fe before I realized it was the pickup guys.

They had been pouring water over my head and soaking my clothes when I asked what had happened to the noon-hour pickup. Everyone started laughing as they told me it was just then noon. Knowing it was my first time out they had come a bit early just in case of some trouble they said.

Some trouble! "I was almost killed three times, and you came 15 minutes early in case of some trouble?" I didn't know if I was mad, sad or happy. Now that I'd lived through it, the trip started to seem a little funny. It was then the driver started telling me about a time schedule they had to maintain to stay safe. He didn't know the details but from 11:00 a.m. until 1:00 p.m. Billy had arranged a guarantee that no cops would be on the pickup road. To me it meant somebody was being paid off somewhere, and that was good. But it also meant if I hadn't been picked up in this two-hour window it would have been the next day before the driver would have come back to get me. I wouldn't have been any better off by then than the guy hanging out in the tree. My luck had been with me the night before and I said another quiet little prayer of gratitude. It seemed I was praying a little more regularly these days.

The job was successful and another one was coming up that was mine for the taking. I told Billy I would have to think about it but it didn't take me long. I had spent my money fast, mostly on entertainment, a good used car and some clothes. Three weeks later I got the call and by then I was broke again. It was up to me, Billy said, this run would pay quite a bit more and I would be the number two man. I liked the idea of working with another more experienced man and later that day I got all the details. This load would be about six times the size of the previous one which meant six times the men. That would be 20 mules, and to me that sounded like a lot of people we had to watch over on that 12-mile walk. While we were going over the final details another man came in who I thought would be my partner for the night. I was shocked to see it was the guy I'd hit in the head with the Frisbee. He was just introduced as Red and I didn't ask any more. When I shook his hand, it was hard to tell if he recognized me from the night at the concert or not. This guy was not only big but also in shape, and his demeanor reminded me a whole lot of old Sam from up at the Green Giant Company, but Red had two arms. He kind of smiled, acted sort of happy, but was a whole lot bad-ass looking, just the type of guy I tried to avoid. To me it was obvious he wasn't showing his true character and I damn sure wasn't going to show mine, so I just nodded and kept quiet. We went over the plan and just like before I would be dropped off, walk through customs, take the same cab to Pasqual's house, and Pasqual would take care of the rest. If I wanted, there could be another load for me to carry, Billy said, but with a laugh I replied "No thanks, I learned my lesson the last time." I would be making enough money from the job, no need to get greedy. Also, with that many unknown men and handling so much pot I thought I'd better keep my wits about me. I was happy to hear my guide would be the same fellow as before, and then I learned my traveling companion wouldn't be Red but my old boss Chuck Biscuit. I'd quit my roofing job with him right after the first run over the border. Chuck and I had talked a couple of times on the phone, but I hadn't seen him much and the relief I felt that it was him going with me and not Red was probably obvious. It turned out Red was in charge of handling the money and any loose ends.

After we were picked up Chuck and I were supposed to return to Tucson and meet Red with the pot at a safe house. Then my job would be done. It sounded easy but so had the first job. The next day went as planned. We were dropped off and walked across the border where the same taxi driver picked us up and delivered us to Pasqual's house. I was starting to like this guy Pasqual. I knew he'd probably kill me if the fancy struck him or I did him wrong, but we just seemed to get along. On this trip I also met his brother who was an altogether different story. It was easy for me to see this guy was nuts. A jittery, nervous type, his laugh alone would scare most people. It made me want to keep him in front of me at all times. Luckily, he wasn't a mule, just another of Pasquale's guys who hung around his house.

That night went smoothly, not at all like the first one. All the mules did their jobs, no snakes or dead men in trees, and I'd rationed my water this time as well. Chuck had even bought an extra canteen of water from the cab driver who I learned also did some smuggling himself. It all went like clockwork. All I had to do was keep my eyes open for trouble and this time we got to the pickup spot right on time. Back in Tucson the drop-off to Red went well, making me think I'd read him wrong. These one-night runs about once a month became my regular job, and I usually would get a phone call a day or two before I was needed. Sometimes I would be alone with a small group of mules; for larger shipments I would have another man with me and not always Chuck. I spent the two or three weeks between jobs swimming or playing basketball at the local YMCA or the city fitness center I had discovered. A party was going on every night somewhere and the music was always good but the crowd just didn't fit me. I got close to a few people but mostly I kept my distance. One morning, after another successful night walking over the border, Red asked me if I would like to accompany him to New York City. There would be three cars: he would be in the lead car, a van would be driven by a married couple, and I would be in the third vehicle, all following each other at 10-mile intervals. Red bought two-way radios so we would be able to communicate in case of cops, and he said he would give me $500 up front for motels, food and gas, telling me to be ready when he called.

It sounded like easy money and I hardly had time to pack before my phone rang. The group was leaving immediately so it was lucky that I had gassed up my car. Red had given me a map showing all the designated fuel stops, motels and even rest areas along our route. For five days straight, we drove and drove until we got to New York, talking on the radio only as necessary. The trip went as smoothly as Red had said it would and by the time I laid up in New York to rest and then drove back to Tucson the whole job took a little over two weeks. These long drives gave me plenty of time to think. I knew I was breaking the law in so many ways but I kept telling myself that I didn't personally handle the pot because the mules and other laborers did the actual hauling. Not that it would make any difference to the cops but I was basically just a security guard.

Late at night out on the United States-Mexican border it wasn't only the Mexican police I had to look out for but other smugglers. They might be hauling weed or exotic birds that brought a lot of money on the U.S. side or any other contraband including people. It wasn't unusual to see a few people crossing the border and at times I had seen dozens all walking in a line carrying bags with everything they owned.

Some had kids with them, others were helping older people. It was sad to witness their pain but these people were never a threat, it was the cocaine smugglers who were the real danger. They would kill us in a heartbeat to protect their goods and steal ours. Billy and Chuck said their mules all carried guns as well. Fortunately, cocaine smugglers usually took a different trail than we did. Their route was several miles further down the border but Chuck had told me that on occasion he had crossed paths with them. "If you run into any of them get away if you can," he warned me, "or if not give them everything you have." My mules would have already dropped their loads and run away so if I was lucky they might only take my money. There was no doubt that this was a risky business and I could already see things could come to an end in a number of different unpleasant ways.

When I wasn't traveling I continued to be a regular at the YMCA and this is where I got to know the real Jonah Martin, the man who I was coming to believe was the boss of this pot running enterprise. Jonah was a big guy with a build like mine but taller and like me he enjoyed working out. A natural athlete, he came to the Y often to play basketball. After discovering his wife and I had met each other years ago back in Oklahoma he invited me to their house for dinner. As I remembered she was a 6'2" redhead with a body like a model and at the time we met she was living with a college friend of mine. We had become friends from the start and had always been able to talk comfortably together. A smart girl with just a little hippie in her and a whole lot of ambition, all the fellows had wanted her. It had been four or five years since Cina and I had spoken and I looked forward to catching up. Cina had been traveling overseas when I met Jonah for the first time during the party at their house so we'd missed each other. Now she and I picked where we'd left off and as I got to know Jonah better, the three of us enjoyed spending time together. A few weeks later they invited me to a Rolling Stones concert treating me to drinks, dinner at a fancy restaurant and a limousine to the show where our seats were two rows from the stage. Afterwards we had backstage passes for a meet-and-greet with the Stones. It was cool.

From the start, Jonah seemed to know a lot about me and my activities and I soon found out how. He clearly had money and lots of it. He owned several exotic cars, big houses in different towns all with big pools, even his own plane. Although he was usually close mouthed about his business dealings, perhaps because of my close relationship with Cina, at times he was a bit talkative with me. I learned he had several businesses and was involved in a film company along with a semi trucking outfit. Cina was also involved in the businesses and would regularly fly somewhere in their plane. I understood from her he had two of them, a prop plane and a jet. They also owned a ski condo in Colorado and a fancy apartment in New York City where they frequently stayed.

This guy Jonah wasn't your average fellow; he was New York City educated, with several degrees and seemed to be involved in a lot of different things. Cina had once mentioned that his father and his father before him had both been very successful New York City lawyers and made a lot of money. Their money had gone into a trust, she told me, and now Jonah, who was an only child, was the heir to it all. I hadn't known Jonah long but from everything Cina said, it sure seemed like he had everything going for him, however, I discovered some strange stuff about him I didn't like. For one thing he hated to lose at anything. It was some kind of obsession with him. If we were flipping a coin to see who bought lunch, if he lost we had to flip again until he won. He also knew about all kinds of sports and he had a knack for winning in just about every event he'd bet on. On the rare occasion that he lost he would double-up on the next bet.

When I saw Red occasionally tagging along with him everything came together: Jonah was the boss of the weed smuggling operation, but why? He didn't need the money; he had money, inherited money and legitimate business money. At his office there were several secretaries working for his film business and several other enterprises including Chuck's roofing company. From a construction company in Seattle to a cattle ranch in New Mexico, he was into all kinds of stuff.

As I hung out with them more, I saw that every Friday a stack of checks went out that stood two feet tall. Many of these people like Red, Billy, Chuck and my three roommates had been working for him for years at times doing legitimate work so why jeopardize it all by smuggling pot? It was a puzzle to me and now he wanted to bring me into his group full time. There would be more money than all my college buddies were making put together. Because Jonah owned the local radio station, perks, like meeting the Rolling Stones, would become a regular thing, and I knew there would be lots of travel because he and Cina went overseas often. All of this would be hard to walk away from. It would be a tough decision and I guess one would call it divine intervention that I didn't have to make that choice because the next day I got a call from my old high school friend Jim Roberds.

Don Irwin, my college roommate from Oklahoma, had been killed in a vehicle-related accident. It wasn't just me, if you were to ask any of our classmates they would all say Don was the nicest guy in our class.

Back in Dewey, when my next-door neighbor Mike Davis moved to Bartlesville, Don had become my new George. We spent nights together, even rode our bikes to school like George and I had, and when I got my first car I went by and picked him up for school every day. Don may not have ever realized it, but over the years I had learned a lot from him about attending class, doing homework, and being more disciplined.

I was getting all the information about the accident from Jim who told me the funeral would be in four days. Don's death brought back feelings I'd almost forgotten. George had left me and now Don had too. I had to go and thought if I hurried I could make it.

Jonah and Cina understood my grief when later that day I declined their job offer and jumped aboard a plane back to Oklahoma, telling them I didn't know when I would be coming back. The loss hit me hard and I never thought of going back to Tucson after the funeral. When I called and told Cina she agreed to take care of everything for me, selling the stuff in my apartment and my car.

I got a job working electrical highline construction in Bartlesville and went back to playing basketball at the local YMCA. Granger Electric did primarily oilfield work and they were very busy. A dozen crews set out from the Bartlesville shop every morning headed for job sites across Washington and Osage counties and up into Kansas, building electric service for wells in remote areas where few people had ever been. Climbing telephone poles in the Oklahoma winter was hard work and the summer was no better when the hot creosote burned your skin and made your eyes water.

After seeing several experienced men slide down "eat a pole" as they say, I knew the job wasn't for me but I stayed on because I'd met a cowboy named Doug Partain who also worked at Granger. Doug was on my crew and he was one of the funniest fellows I'd ever known. He was also an awesome calf roper and hoping to go pro, so on weekends he competed in every small-town rodeo he could find to improve his roping skills. A few days after we met he invited me to watch him practice at his house. Through Doug I met other rodeo cowboys and that started my short-lived career as a bulldogger, a rodeo event which requires a cowboy to ride his horse alongside a steer, jump off and wrestle the steer to the ground. Like Doug, these guys practiced hard every night regardless of the weather because most of the arenas where rodeos were held were uncovered so you needed to be prepared for every kind of condition, rain or shine, day or night.

I bought myself a good horse which is essential in bulldogging and she quickly established a reputation for herself on the rodeo circuit, becoming known simply as "Mare." With this horse I was immediately welcomed by other rodeo contestants who wanted to compete on her. In steer wrestling if you borrow a man's horse and win, you give a share of the prize money to the horse's owner. I traveled to a lot of rodeos and although I wasn't doing that great personally, a lot of good cowboys were riding my horse so "Mare" was paying the bills.

It had been two years since Don had died. Bulldogging had helped me put his death behind me but I wasn't fully over it when another in our pack of five was killed in a single car accident. Jim Roberds had lived three houses down from me and had been the smartest of our bunch. We had talked some after I came back to Oklahoma but hadn't really kept up with each other since Don's funeral. Now Jim was gone. I hit the rodeo circuit hard and that horse and I traveled as far as my gas money would take us. One week we'd be in Texas, the next

Missouri and after that Colorado. I wound up blowing out my knee in Wichita, Kansas, and while I was recovering, I had to sell my horse and trailer along with all of my rodeo gear.

After rehab a construction job kept me going during the day and at night I cleaned a beauty shop where my mother worked in the Price Tower in Bartlesville. The owner, Barbara Curtis had been married to a famous rodeo stock contractor named Eddie Curtis. As a boy I had often visited their ranch and had loved his stories about the rodeo.

That job along with a part-time job as a bouncer at a music hall along with some security work for concerts was entertaining for a while, but still preoccupied by the deaths of my friends, I got bored easily. My daytime job in construction got a little more interesting when out of the blue I was asked for a personal favor by the boss's son Ron. He was a guy my age whose grandfather had started the company more than 50 years before, and now his dad was teaching him how to run it. It seemed he and a few of his college fraternity brothers had recently attended a Texas Rangers baseball game where they had season tickets. Ron admitted that they always drank too much beer at these games and while walking back to their car three scruffy-looking guys approached them demanding beer. He said it became obvious they wouldn't leave them alone until they gave them the beer, so they did. Ron and his buddies had seen these guys before at games, and thought they would be waiting for them at their car again after the next game. He told me he and his friends weren't going to be intimidated and he had a couple of other fraternity brothers planning to meet them there. He wanted me to come along as back up just in case there was trouble. I knew Ron pretty well after working with him over the past year and had also run into a few of his fraternity brothers. Most of them were in good shape but I could tell they weren't fighters. Deep down I think Ron knew it too and I realized if it came down to it, fighting would be my job.

With the promise of some extra money, three days later we were driving to Dallas for the next game and I got a bit more of the story. It had happened somewhat like Ron had said, but he and his friends might have started the whole thing. After listening to his story, I was sure the three guys would be waiting for them after the game. As usual for their group during the game the beer flowed fueling brave talk among the boys about their upcoming encounter. I wasn't feeling so confident and I didn't think I would have any backup if these guys turned out to be real bad asses. During the game I didn't do any drinking and stayed behind the group. Walking back to the car there were no signs of the three men everyone had been so worried about and the next thing I knew Ron and his buddies were all singing their fraternity fight song in harmony. They popped the trunks of their cars where ice chests were full of more beer, and a new party started.

I was relaxing in the back seat of the car, which was parked several parking spaces away from the group's party, when from a distance I saw three men walking toward the partiers. It had to be the three he had told me about and as they got closer I could see these weren't boys; they were older than me by a long way. They weren't your average type of street people as Ron had told me they were either. They looked tough. As the group caught sight of them, I could see right off this wasn't going to be good.

Not an experienced fighter, Ron led with his face first, right into a fist. After a drop kick followed by a couple of shots to his gut he was on the ground. Two of his friends could offer little help as they too were getting the bad end of the whooping and the others were at a distance yelling for the three guys to stop. This group of eight bad-ass college ruffians had been reduced to three bloody boys in no time at all. Not in a big hurry to get into their mess, as I got out of the car surveying the situation I grabbed a golf club from the open trunk and went to the driver's side of the car and started honking that horn. I honked it a dozen times until I got the attention of the three who by now were really putting a hurt on any of the boys they could get their hands on. Things ended quickly when they saw me walking toward them with the golf club swung back in striking position. When I told them the cops were on the way they split and I felt lucky. Just as suddenly I had eight boys surrounding me calling me a hero. Ron was thankful but he just wanted to go home. His face was a mess with a busted lip, a bad gash on his forehead and several other cuts, but after looking him over I told him he was going to be okay. Nonetheless he wanted me to drive him home so he could be checked out by his own doctor in Bartlesville. He had learned a valuable lesson the hard way. Despite some bruised ribs and a deflated ego, he was fortunate. After that day I could do no wrong with Ron or his parents. The family took me under their wing and I frequently went on skiing trips and other vacations with them, considering them to be my second family.

After that weekend it seemed like once a month one of his fraternity brothers would call with some kind of problem they thought I could help with. I hauled horses to Tennessee for one guy's girlfriend and found a stolen dog for another. No job was too small if it paid. Although I was rarely putting in a 40-hour week, I was still working construction for Ron when once again he approached me with a sensitive problem. Someone was sending letters to the local newspaper accusing him of belonging to a secret club when he was in high school called the "White Knights." The letter claimed that he and several other prominent kids in the club had raped a girl who was now the anonymous letter writer's wife.

It was quite a story and when Ron showed me a copy of one of the letters that the newspaper had received, I found it hard to absorb. These events would have taken place 25 years before when the victim was allegedly 14 years old. Ron, who was now married with kids, swore he was innocent and I honestly believed him. He was about as green behind the ears about girls as anyone I'd ever seen and I doubted he'd ever been to bed with anyone except his wife. Of course, there was no signature on the letters or return address on the envelopes so I didn't know what to tell him.

The next morning my phone rang before I was up. More letters had been sent, including to the police and the local radio station. Ron was calling his lawyer next and wanted to know what I thought. I wanted to help him and decided to re-read the letters. When I did the last name of another of the "White Knights" caught my attention and he turned out to be the son of a prominent local lawyer.

Denny Garrison was a well-established attorney with a big practice in Bartlesville, who a few years back had come close to being elected governor of Oklahoma. At a meeting I arranged with him, Denny told me the letters were also accusing his son of being a member of the White Knights. Denny was as mad as a man could get. Like Ron he wanted to know who was sending the letters and where he lived and he said he would take care of the rest.

That afternoon I got a call from a detective in the Bartlesville Police Department who was also trying to identify and locate the letter writer. All we had to go on was that the letters had been postmarked in California. The more recent letters had taken an increasingly violent tone, with threats of reprisals against supposed members of the White Knights. Then a letter arrived giving the first name of the girl who supposedly had been attacked. After digging through several old yearbooks, I located her photo and found several of her classmates. After that I figured things out. Wesley, as he was called, was also harassing one of these women, and her husband wanted to find him, offering me money to tell him where the culprit lived. Like Denny, the husband, who was a cattle rancher, didn't know anything about the guy. When his wife started to get phone calls as well as letters, he too became infuriated.

I found Wesley was threatening about half a dozen people in town with crazy accusations and they were all desperate to find out who he was and if he was dangerous or just some kind of nut. I had a dilemma. I thought if I revealed the guy's identity to either the rancher or Denny, one of them might do something he would regret later. As for the cops, I didn't think they could act unless Wesley actually hurt someone.

I would have to meet with him myself and through his mother who lived in Bartlesville, I learned he planned to be in Oklahoma the following week. I decided to keep Wesley's identity to myself so as not to spook him and made plans to cross paths with him at a local bar where I had heard he liked to hang out. I hoped to build a relationship that would allow me to evaluate him and then decide what would be best to do. Over the next few weeks we ate and drank together on several occasions. President of his high school class and a college graduate, he turned out to be a very smart person. When I had gained his confidence he gradually began to speak openly about the letters he had sent to all the White Knights and the rancher's wife, bragging that no one knew who he was. After about a dozen conversations, I had enough. I told him he was way off base with all his accusations and I would have to go to the police if he didn't stop.

That would be the end of our relationship and before long another batch of letters arrived saying that I was a member of the White Knights too, claiming that I was their hitman and cocaine supplier. The letters didn't bother me in the least, I thought they were almost comical. My part of the investigation was over and with my help the cops were on to Wesley. However, after a lengthy interview with his wife in California they decided he was not a danger, just someone who needed to take his medication regularly to function. When he didn't he was prone to wild fantasies which had led to these problems. The last I heard, his wife had promised the cops to do the best she could to get him back on track. After what I had learned about Wesley, I told Ron I didn't think she'd have much luck.

Lots of Honest Work

I'd been back in my hometown for two years and had worked at a little bit of everything. At the urging of two-time Board President Derry Ebert, I was appointed to the Board of Directors at the Bartlesville YMCA and quickly became Vice President of the Board. I was also serving as President of the Board of Adjustments for Washington County and before long I was frustrated with both positions. I had limited experience with any kind of governance but I also had no tolerance for bad management and waste. I soon found myself in hot water with both organizations for outspokenness and after serving out my terms I resigned from both Boards.

Once more I was ready for a change. I had already given my notice to Ron when I heard that the Tulsa fairgrounds was looking for security guards for a new horse-racing track that would be open soon. It sounded interesting and I was hired the same day I applied with a guarantee that I could start work the next day if I wanted.

My new boss at the fairgrounds turned out to be Rod Shotts, a very well-known former college football star from the University of Oklahoma, and we got along fine from day one. Being single, I worked whenever I was called, which was often, and by everyone. If a food vendor needed something I got a call. Delivery truck drivers had my number as did many of the horse owners and trainers. I was on call so much Rod allowed me to put a small camper on site just so I was close by. If I wasn't hauling money to the bank or horse piss to Oklahoma City for testing, I was interviewing bands to play between races. I also got some good side jobs that often popped up. After guarding some fancy multi-million-dollar cars that were never to be left alone during a car show at the Tulsa State Fair I got a reputation for dependability when no one showed up for a shift change. These cars were locked up in a trailer in a secure building on the fairgrounds and I could have easily left after my shift. It was a good thing that I stayed because one of the owners popped in unexpectedly in the middle of the night. When the next shift guard didn't show, I stayed again. For 24 hours I stayed. When the owner showed up again and learned of my efforts my reward was not only cash but a job offer. I had plenty of work and was happy where I was, but I took his number. Rod also brought me opportunities to go out on the road, some of which I took. In Chapel Hill, North Carolina I worked undercover while looking for a runaway kid. I worked for the Price Pipeline Company looking for theft in Paris, Texas. A stolen construction truck loaded with tools took me across three states before I located it. If I wasn't working I was sleeping.

It was after one of these odd jobs that I met Charlie Mitchell, a famous soccer player from Scotland who was a friend of the racetrack manager. Mitchell knew about me from Ron, and I was about to learn more about him. Charlie had played for the New York Cosmos and the Tulsa Roughnecks. After retiring, he had opened up several fish and chips restaurants in Tulsa and the surrounding area. Although I was busy at the time, I felt a little honored when shortly after we met he said he could use my help. After speaking with Ron, I made myself available and quickly learned that my job for this Scotsman would have several parts, all of which were equal.

First was security. There had been a couple of fights lately at the bar-restaurant he just opened at the racetrack which was hurting its image. The manager didn't seem able to do much about it and Charlie was just too busy to hang out there all of the time.

Second was theft. Somebody was robbing him blind at another restaurant he had in Tulsa, and it seemed like there had been a lot of food unaccounted for lately. Charlie had also just opened the first sports café in the state with dozens of televisions. He wanted me to work with the manager there to organize the security for this place as well.

It would be an open-ended job reporting to several restaurant managers and unless I had something Charlie wouldn't ask any questions. I liked the idea and soon I was officially on his payroll listed as restaurant help. From washing dishes to making salads, I became a jack of all trades, wrapping potatoes, hauling out the trash at night and mopping the floors. If they were shorthanded, some mornings I'd come in early to vacuum the dining room or maybe wash windows. I didn't ask questions or snoop around, I just showed up on time and did whatever was needed. I quickly learned that in the food industry it is common for people to show up late or quit without notice. It is hard to find and keep kitchen help and several weeks into the job I found myself working at any of Charlie's restaurants that needed me.

The job at the fairgrounds was still working out so sometimes I was getting paid both while working at the track and while keeping my eyes open at Charlie's restaurant. I was on the job somewhere 24 hours a day. It didn't take long to fit in with the restaurant employees and soon I started seeing one of the waitresses who I really took a liking to.

It came as a complete surprise to me when she mentioned one of the managers had some frozen shrimp for sale. I immediately told her to get us a box or two, giving her the money plus a little extra. I was enjoying spending time with this new girlfriend of mine and hoped it would turn out she wasn't involved, but when I ordered more the next week I knew she was. This was downright theft and although I didn't want to, I had to tell Charlie. After I placed a couple more food orders, the soccer player had seen enough and one day the manager and the waitress were nowhere to be seen. Rumors spread around the restaurant that they had both been arrested and were in jail. Probably for the best, I would never see her again.

It was a sad couple of months for me. I kept on working for Charlie and keeping my eyes open for other thefts, but a bit broken hearted, I'd had my fill of it.

Between Charlie, who had contacts all over the world, and Ron who had his own network through OU and the racetrack, I was still getting all kinds of job offers. After obtaining the required licenses, I started doing courier work of all kinds, even escorting an elderly couple to visit their son in Jamaica. It was all first class. I just laid in the sun all day at a five-star hotel ordering room service. Then several days later I took them home.

I kept some part time work going at the fairgrounds where my camper was still parked but most of the time I was busy with other projects. Ron was always easy to work with and Denny, the general manager was especially good to me. Denny supervised every operation on the property from the Tulsa State Fair to the race track and dozens of trade shows. He had a big job and after I caught two of his people stealing on the grounds we became friends.

In the 1980s Tulsa had its share of gangs and at night the back streets around the fairgrounds were full of trouble. Theft, violence, even murder was common. This wasn't unique to Tulsa but that's where I was calling home and with no perimeter fence the fairgrounds were easy pickings. Tulsa County had one-night security guard assigned to the property and he had a radio that went straight to other deputies but one man could not properly cover over a hundred acres full of dozens of buildings at night. When my truck was parked by the camper he knew he had someone close by if he needed help which was another reason I was allowed to keep my camper there.

It was Denny who told me about a college buddy of his in Dallas who was looking for someone he could trust. Nothing was keeping me in Tulsa so when Denny told me a second time how much his friend could use my help, I took the number and called him. This was another case of theft but this time it wasn't food. Someone was stealing money from an historic nightclub this fellow owned and he needed help investigating the thefts. Based on our conversation and Denny's wholehearted recommendation, he immediately hired me over the phone.

This sounded like another job where I would be on site all the time so when I arrived in Dallas I looked for a place to live close by the club. It was located on what locals commonly called Lower Greenville, a neighborhood near the campus of Southern Methodist University. I could tell most nights it was half full of students and the other half was working adults, most looking for a good time. There were also quite a few street people who were around late at night, making Lower Greenville a busy place 24 hours a day. Older apartment buildings were plentiful in the area and if you didn't mind sharing a bathroom they were cheap. I checked out the neighborhood several times, driving the route between the club and the apartments, figuring no farther than it was I could walk it for the exercise. Single and with no steady girl to impress, I found a semi-furnished unit with a month-to-month agreement just in case things didn't work out. I'd been in town a week when I gave my new boss a call.

His name was Brent Wacom and over lunch in a restaurant near the club he gave me the details about my new position. As it turned out he was just one of the partners in a nightclub business called Nick's Uptown. Among the four other partners was the son of the original owner of Six Flags Amusement Park. This caught my interest right away because as a young boy my parents had taken me to the new (at the time) theme park. Jumping on a French riverboat, taking my first gondola ride and seeing the Wild West shows at the park were some of the best memories from my youth. Taking this job was going to be a trip down memory lane and

I planned to go to Six Flags as soon as I could.

Our initial meeting quickly turned into my first day of work when as we were walking back to the club from lunch, B.B. King's tour bus turned into the back-parking lot of Nick's. The coach doors opened and we were invited into where King sat. By now I'd worked with some well-known folks in my life, and my experiences in Tucson with Jonah, going to big-name shows and often meeting the performers, had made me a bit nonchalant about celebrities but it was still a thrill shooting the breeze with the King. I was introduced as the man with all the answers: If they needed anything, see Dale. What the hell was he talking about? I thought to myself as Brent stepped off the bus handing me a set of keys along with the name of the bar manager who he said would be in shortly. It would be the last I saw of him until show time that evening.

As the stage crew set up and more people started showing up for work, including the bar manager, it was easy to see that this place needed help. Nothing had been cleaned from the night before, from dirty glasses on the tables to filthy bathrooms, the place was a mess and smelled even worse. My first job would be to make sure that the club was clean when I left at night after the last show.

Five nights a week some big-name entertainer would show up, do the show, and be gone that evening to another venue. Nick's was a stopping spot for these acts and had been an entertainment landmark for years. I was there when the tour buses arrived and I waved goodbye and locked the doors when they left. Catering to thousands of students in the area the Greenville strip turned out to be almost two miles of solid bars and restaurants and Nick's was the most popular of them all.

According to what Brent had told me someone was stealing from Nick's but he hadn't given me many details. I was to find out whatever I could and report only to him. To everyone else I would just be the janitor and part-time doorman who had the keys to the building. It seemed kind of strange that his partners weren't involved in our relationship but the money was good and the benefits were even better. My access to every celebrity that came through Nick's doors made me very popular with the female clientele although I was usually too busy to take advantage of it. The constant schedule of show after show kept me occupied, getting to the club early and leaving late. After several weeks I got to know all the staff and quickly spotted how the club was being ripped off. But when I gave Brent a report he told me this pocket-change theft wasn't what he was looking for. A lot more money missing than a couple of bartenders stealing a little cash out of a register could account for. So far that was all I had been able to uncover so he promoted me to assistant manager, where I got to actually handle money and count the night's receipts. This way I could follow the money trail, and two weeks later that's what I was doing.

The security situation at Nick's was in good shape. Besides me, a black dude named Martin was my regular guy and extra muscle if I needed it. He was usually friendly with people but if things got nasty, which every once in a while, they did, Martin was "the Man." From the first day I determined that he was an honest guy and my instincts turned out to be true. The general manger seemed to be okay as well although he did drink too much. Though the waitresses were giving away too many drinks for extra tips, this was a common thing waitresses did in most clubs and I just didn't see any big money being stolen.

I'd been at Nick's six months before Brent's mystery was solved, and when it did Dallas lost a landmark. Drugs were fairly common in the rock and roll music industry, and it wasn't unusual for me to see pot or cocaine passed around between the musicians and staff. No one got fired for it, and so far, no one had been canned for stealing either. Because I was still a bit of an outsider, the "new guy" as they still called me, I just wasn't in the real thick of things and it didn't help that I didn't indulge in their cocaine snorting. What I was into was working out, keeping my eyes open at the bar, and chasing a few girls. And it would be the girls that opened Brent's eyes as to where his lost money was going.

Phoebe was a beautiful girl who by anyone's standards was a "10." She was a regular at the club who at times had her nose in the air, nevertheless, any man would pay to be with her and she knew it. Her personality ran hot and cold, sometimes sweet and at other times standoffish but she was so beautiful she got away with it. She also could be a bit of a drinker, and when she did drink someone usually got lucky. One night when Asleep at the Wheel was playing that someone was me. Unfortunately, it wasn't sex I was after but the information I was sure she had. I noticed she seemed to have access to the manager's private office on occasion and since she wasn't an employee she shouldn't have been in there. This was the area where all the cash and receipts were stored and it was the one place even I didn't have a key to. I had been in the room a few times with Brent so I knew the door could be locked from the inside meaning I was never actually able to catch what was going on. However, lately I had seen Phoebe going into the office on a regular basis and I was getting curious. As I had hoped on this night she talked.

For several weeks afterwards I partied with staff, doing whatever it took to get the information I needed. From waitresses to bartenders to the manager himself and even some of the customers, everyone was doing white powder, and I found out the guy supplying them was one of Brent's partners. A short, thin fellow at our weekly employee meetings he'd always been distant to me. His quirky attitude made him hard to read at first, but not now. It was clear he had been dealing out of the club and using money from the partnership to finance it all.

The rest came both easy and hard for Brent and me, as he

investigated my findings further. I stayed with him while the club fulfilled the remaining contracts and after that the partnership was dissolved and everything was sold. Despite losing a lot of money Brent was very generous to me; he was a good guy in the wrong business who treated me very fairly. He even offered me another job but I felt my time in Dallas had come to an end. I was disappointed that so many good people I'd met and worked with got caught up in it all.

I was playing basketball at one of the Dallas YMCAs and thinking about going back to Oklahoma when another opportunity came up. I'd met Joe in the gym after a pickup game several weeks earlier and he mentioned he was looking for some men for a job he had in the works. A cathodic protection engineer, Joe's company sent crews of men out checking pipelines around the country for bad spots. This involved two men walking the pipeline, one carrying a metal detector and the other carrying a probing rod which sent a signal to a third man who was reading an instrument back at the truck. The information was then sent to Dallas where Joe translated it and sent the results to the owner of the pipeline. The crews themselves didn't particularly know anything about the equipment. Their job was just to walk the pipeline and probe he surface of the ground above it.

Joe told me he needed a foreman to supervise these walkers. He had a big job coming up that would stretch from Houston, Texas, to Chicago, Illinois, and would take close to a year, he calculated. Now that I was out of work I called him and over lunch the next day we talked more. I agreed to start the following week, which was actually perfect because I'd already given my 30-day notice on my apartment. I rented a small storage unit for my stuff, and for the next year I planned on living in a motel.

BEFORE THE DEW

Motels and Diners

A couple weeks of training at Joe's office was all it took for me to get a handle on the job. You needed to keep the equipment clean and be sure to hook up the wiring right and you walked a lot. While he was training me, Joe ran an ad for help in the local paper interviewing several dozen applicants, many who weren't in good enough shape to walk the distance day after day. Others were obvious drunks or had personal problems of some kind, however we did find some good ones we thought would work out. All four of the pipelines started in Houston, Texas, lying side by side most of the way to Chicago so I would need 12 men in my crew, three to a line. After a few days of training, the men and I hit the road in four SUVs packed with gear.

The first couple of weeks everything went well, then payday hit. We weren't that far out of Houston when one man just disappeared. We had all stayed at a Motel 8 and the morning after payday he was gone. Most of the guys were right out of high school or college dropouts but this guy was older, maybe 45 or 50. I didn't suspect any foul play and neither did Joe when I called him about it. For the next two days we just kept going, one man short, which meant I walked the pipeline, something I actually enjoyed. When Joe brought another man for the crew we both realized it wouldn't be the last time he'd have to do that.

I hadn't expected it but the men were more trouble than the job itself. Some of them would spent all their money at bars on payday and were broke all week; some got homesick and others couldn't take the walking. It got to where I was always short a man or two.

Spending money on liquor and pot wasn't for me, but I didn't object to their indulgence as long as they got up in the morning and did their jobs. Joe would have to send me more men as time went on and bus them to me as we traveled farther from Houston. I treated them fairly but it felt like every payday for some reason somebody quit. Days off were few and we usually worked from sunup to sundown. The equipment couldn't get wet so if it rained the guys got time off. There was no full day off for me, rainy days meant getting caught up on paper-work. Marching like soldiers nothing stopped us but rain, and did we pray for rain on occasion. We were a third of the way through the job when Joe informed me we were ahead of schedule which meant bonuses. I only had three of the original 12 men left on the crew but everyone would get some extra money including me.

I was happy about the extra money but I was also looking forward to finishing the job. I liked the traveling but this project had turned out to be quite an ordeal at times. I had to deal with the men and all their problems including two runaway girls showing up in one guy's motel room. Then there was the job itself and all of the paperwork. I'd about had my fill and still had six months to go. A few days off along the way would have been nice, but between keeping track of the 12 workers and paying for everything out on the road there just wasn't any time to take off. Nonetheless, I'd promised Joe a year of my time and I intended to stick to my word.

To keep the men motivated I promised more bonus checks and tried to step up the pace as much as I could. They got paid by the hour and I got'em up early every day. Some whined but others were ready to go, wanting that money. If you were hung over you worked or got fired. If you were sick you worked or went to the local town doctor. By the time we could see the lights of Chicago in the night sky most of the men wanted me dead but funny how a fat paycheck changed that. In a few more days the job was over and the guys who had stuck it out with me went home happy. I had seen a lot of the country and now that the job was finished I was happy too. Joe made some money and he was happy as well. He also had another job coming up for me but after a year on the road I was ready to go home.

Back in Oklahoma with a pocket full of money I didn't have any trouble when it came to spending it. Within a few weeks I had a truck and an apartment in Tulsa. After my friend Charlie Mitchell gave me a job in another new sports bar and grill he had just opened it felt like I'd never left. My arrangement with Denny to keep my camper at the fairgrounds had collapsed 6 months earlier when he died. I was told it was a massive heart attack right there on the fairgrounds. It had been a good ride working for him and Ron at the fairgrounds and I had made a lot of good contacts. I had no regrets except for Denny's death. He was just 40 years old with kids and I felt like once again death had stolen someone close to me way before their time.

I settled in working for Charlie but it wasn't long before I started to think about traveling again. This time I didn't want to stay in hotels or pull a trailer. I wanted something I could live in and I thought a motor coach would be the most practical idea. I'd been looking around at used motor coaches when my cousin called me from Seneca, Missouri, about one that sounded too good to be true. I was planning to visit him anyway so I immediately jumped into my truck and headed up Highway 244 toward his place which was about three hours away. It turned out the motor home was not what I was looking for but when he asked me to stay for a few days, I jumped all over it. I'd stayed in this area many times in my life, starting as a kid when my uncle lived here. There were a couple of old time family members buried in the city cemetery whose graves I also wanted to visit. After calling back to Tulsa to make sure I wouldn't be missed, I started looking forward to a few days off. This land wasn't farmland like back home and, with all the rolling hills and brush, not particularly good for cattle. What I liked about the area was the remoteness. I could take about any gravel road off the main highway and within a mile or two I felt like I was far from civilization. People that didn't know their way around were regularly getting lost, and I did myself the first day I was there. While I was exploring I learned that property was really cheap, especially way out in the country. During one of these drives with my cousin looking at land for sale, the name Damon Anderson came up in my cousin's conversation.

The property we were looking at that particular day was 10 acres with a couple of small rolling hills loaded with trees. A house sat on the next piece of land that looked like maybe 50 acres, and after that we really started getting out in the sticks. My cousin lived not far down the road and knew about the property because a friend of his at church wanted to sell it. As we walked the fence line around the property he told me who all the neighbors were and what he knew about them. It was on the south side fence he first mentioned the name Anderson. He said Anderson had apparently moved into the area 15 or 16 years earlier and my cousin didn't know if he actually owned the house and property or not. He was a handy guy. My cousin knew that for a fact as he said Anderson had done some welding work for him a few years back remembering that the guy had a real mean dog. He didn't see him around town much except at the grocery store and other than that he thought Anderson just stayed at home working in a shop that sat at the back of the property.

From the physical description he gave me it sounded like all the wanted posters that hung around Oklahoma for years with the name Damon "Chub" Anderson on them. Right height and weight with a muscular build and when my cousin mentioned the name Chub it all came together. I didn't think I'd ever seen the guy in person but I for sure had heard of the murder of E.C. Mullendore III. When I was a 14 year old back in the 1960s working as a bus boy at the Embers Restaurant in Bartlesville, the Mullendore family had come in often to eat, and I'd met E.C. many times. I was a senior in high school when E.C. was killed on September 26, 1970 and remembered it well. Damon Anderson had been the only other person with E.C. on the night of the murder and I'd heard he was somebody you didn't mess with. Although there was a reward for information leading to his capture on pot cultivation charges, this guy had done nothing to me. If he was the kind of person people said he was, I also didn't want my cousin or his family getting involved, maybe even turning him in. I decided it would be best to keep what I knew to myself and after looking over the land I told him it wasn't what I was looking for and just let it go.

A month passed when I got a call from my cousin about a big arrest that made the local paper in Seneca. He said three bail bondsmen from Oklahoma City had all the local and state police there and arrested the Anderson guy he had been telling me about. My cousin was all excited because the authorities had found some sort of Mach 10 machine gun along with a bunch of pot all bound up ready for sale. Now the whole town was talking about the Mullendore murder and who Damon Anderson was.

When I drove to Seneca supposedly for a look at another piece of property that was for sale I heard the whole story. The three bondsmen from Oklahoma, John Dawson, Charles Sellers, and John Van Pelt, had called in the cops thinking they had finally caught the real Chub Anderson. After fingerprinting the character, they found out the fellow's real name wasn't Damon Anderson but a convicted felon trying to hide from the police. Why someone would use such a high-profile name like Damon Anderson's who had been wanted by the law for years I'd never know but for months afterward my cousin would call me every time a new rumor cropped up about the murder. I knew that through the years the Mullendore murder had kept people's interest, especially because it was unsolved but I was too busy to dwell on it.

BEFORE THE DEW

Lucky to Quit When I Did

I was working a security job for country music singer Michael Martin Murphey at Woolaroc, a fantastic museum and wildlife preserve outside of Bartlesville, when I got the idea to go into the buffalo business. Like many people I'd always been fascinated with buffalo and their history. Just the sight of these magnificent creatures was awe inspiring. I had always wanted a full head mount but as they were costly and I rarely had a permanent home to hang one in, it just didn't make sense to spend the money.

After Murphey's concert when I went to Denver to provide security for another act at a big stock show I got to visiting with the owner of a nationwide chain of travel convenience centers about buffalo. He too liked buffalo and had always wanted to sell full buffalo mounts at his stores but could never find a supplier that could price them well enough so he could make a little money. During the seven-day show we spoke several times and I took his number. I'd read in a trade magazine that because of financial difficulties a Native American Indian tribe in South Dakota was selling off a bunch of their buffalo and on a whim, I called them for more information. I was already in Denver and the price they were quoting me for full grown buffalo bulls I just couldn't believe. Two days later I was in South Dakota looking at hundreds of them.

They were something to see, but this was crazy and I knew it. I guess I just wanted a little vacation but it was worth the trip I told the fellow showing me around. I'd been snooping around for a couple of hours watching the cowboys load several semi stock trailers with buffalo when I got curious and asked where all of them were being shipped. He said these buffalo and a lot more were going to a slaughter house in Iowa. TV mogul Ted Turner had purchased a lot of the buffalo to fulfill a contract with the Navy to supply meat to U.S. ships overseas and the closest USDA authorized slaughter house big enough to handle all these buffalo was in Iowa.

I was asking too many questions for my own good. After finding out the shipping costs I made a few phone calls, including one to my new buddy from the stock show. The next day I was standing on a high platform selecting 20 big bulls that would be the start of my new business selling buffalo mounts and hides. The Native American drivers of the big rigs who were all independent owners and anxious for another job, easily guaranteed the delivery date I needed. I'd already gotten prices from the packing plant, informing them another truck would soon be coming with my buffalo. That gave me a little more time to work out some of the finer details of the enterprise I'd just gotten myself into and it was a good thing. Four days later I was in McPherson, Kansas watching half a dozen Mexican workers at the slaughter house do their job, informing them that I wanted the hides cut cleanly with no holes or cut marks. With the precision of a surgeon within eight hours they had the 20 hides loaded up and ready to go in a stock trailer I'd brought with me. The meat itself would hang at the slaughterhouse for seven days curing, but these hides had to be frozen before they spoiled, and that was my job. I was taking them to one of the best-known taxidermists in the country who just happened to live in Oklahoma and had a giant walk-in freezer.

An hour into the trip I was checking the trailer to make sure the tires were okay when I noticed a heavy trail of blood behind me. To make matters worse, it started snowing, making the blood trail even more visible. I hadn't expected the hides to retain so much blood and knew I had to be breaking some kind of law but luckily, I was never pulled over. After driving all night, I showed up at Jim's Heads and Hides Taxidermy just as the sun was coming up and he was waiting for me.

It would take several weeks before I saw my first mount, and it was a beauty. By then I wasn't just trying to sell buffalo mounts but also buffalo meat. The meat I got from the slaughter house was all USDA inspected and put into one-pound packages and at a dollar per pound it was selling well. My problem was I had underestimated how much meat would come from 20 bulls and despite selling a lot, my inventory wasn't going down fast enough. I was paying for freezer space in two places, one in Iowa where I still had the bulk of the meat and another in nearby Caney, Kansas, where I kept several hundred pounds. Fortunately, when I told my Iowa butcher about my excess meat I learned that Ted Turner was short on one of his shipments and would pay the going rate for the rest of what I had. This meant I would come out just about even on the meat, but I still had the hides which was what I had wanted to start with. During the transaction I also made a deal to buy some of Turner's hides bringing my total to over 50. The taxidermist was overwhelmed. It took some time to do a good job on just one and to get them all done quickly I was soon calling taxidermists around the state and also spending a lot of money.

As the buffalo heads started coming my way, about one a week, it was off to the new owners I would go, usually delivering the head myself. These things were so big they wouldn't fit in the biggest car so for a small additional fee I was always glad to transport them. Texas, Nebraska, even a couple to New York, I was on the road again. Before long buffalo orders started dropping off but the problem was those buffalo mounts were still coming now about two a week. My Denver stock show connection did take some which I was happy to deliver to his stores but they were scattered all over the Southwest and it took a lot of time. The mounts he ordered filled a whole six-horse trailer and it took me two weeks to deliver them all.

My last delivery was to a big truck plaza and visitors center in Santa Fe where I planned to visit my friend Cina. Although I had talked to her by phone a few times it had been close to six years since I'd last seen Jonah and Cina and all I knew was that they still were living in Santa Fe. After I arrived in town and delivered the last of the buffalo I gave Cina a call. I immediately felt something was up when she didn't invite me over and instead arranged to meet me at a restaurant on the town square.

Jonah and Cina were very successful at everything they did and their business interests went far beyond smuggling pot. While I was waiting for her to arrive I kept hoping the problem was not too serious, like maybe one of her two kids wasn't doing well in school. I knew they owned a couple of houses along with a nice restaurant in the heart of town yet for some reason she didn't suggest meeting me at any of those places. Perhaps they were having difficulty with the restaurant. All of this was going through my mind when Cina arrived and I learned that the problem was much worse.

Cina had just been released after a two-day interrogation, and when she went home the cops were there boxing up and hauling off all of her office paperwork, tearing the house up while doing it. They confiscated everything of value. All her bank accounts were frozen and she had no cash at all.

When I asked about Jonah she said that to protect the kids they had secretly divorced three years ago and all she knew was what the cops had told her during the interrogation. He and 42 of his employees from around the country had all been arrested at the same time and now were being held on a variety of drug charges. One of the cops had said it had been a two-year federal investigation into Jonah and all his businesses. The only reason she figured they had let her go was because they were divorced. Now more mad than sad about her situation Cina said she'd gotten out of Jonah's life after the divorce and knew very little about his business dealings. The divorce had been finalized and she had broken all their ties except when it came to the kids. Apparently, the cops didn't go for it and they were going to make her explain how she made her living and document how every single thing she had was paid for.

Cina was worn out and there was little I could do to help except give her most of the cash I had with me along with some moral support. I tried to reassure her that everything would work out and then I had to hit the road. When I stopped for fuel on the way out of town I picked up an Albuquerque newspaper and the bust was right on the front page. Like Cina had said, it had been a two-year federal investigation and at precisely 2 p.m. around the country 42 people including some women and an underage girl carrying over a million dollars in cash were arrested. Jonah, who the paper said was the mastermind, was being held without bond in the county jail. The list of confiscated items filled a whole page: millions of dollars in cash, airplanes, semi-trucks, cars, boats, and houses, several in different states. The cops also raided a couple of Albuquerque's best-known music clubs which Jonah owned. It was a major bust all right and the next day when I found another Albuquerque newspaper there it was on the front page again with photos showing the cops closing down Cina's restaurant. The article also listed all the people who had been arrested, many of whom I knew. I felt lucky to have gotten out when I did.

Meanwhile I had my own problems. Those buffalo were still coming and my sales had dwindled down to nothing. I'd flooded the market but I still had 15 mounts which added up to around $30,000 in inventory. Back home, I was making a lot of phone calls along with in-person sales visits without any luck and I was going broke. Six months went by and when I'd only sold a couple of mounts I got an idea. In Santa Fe I'd noticed a corner of a busy intersection where Mexicans sold everything from jewelry to dirt. The last time I had stopped there, they had been selling plants, homemade clothes, wooden posts and everything in between. It also seemed there was no kind of license required. Desperate, I kept thinking maybe it would be a good spot to set up and sell some of these damn buffalo mounts.

It had been close to a year since I had seen or heard from Cina so I had no idea if she was free or in jail, but I was sure whatever was going on wasn't good. Loading up my trailer, hopefully for the last time, when I got to Santa Fe I found out that she still had her house but was losing it too. All the nice paintings, the pool table, even the yard ornaments were all gone. It had been a fairy tale story and when the bell struck two p.m. everything had come tumbling down. Now she was working two jobs to get by and even with that things were a struggle for her. Cina told me that Jonah had been found guilty and was serving his time in a Colorado prison. Half of the 42 arrested had rolled over on him in exchange for lighter sentences but Jonah had not cooperated. According to Cina, he stood straight up in the courtroom and told the judge he would not betray his friends.

At close to 60 years old, Jonah received a 20-year sentence which meant with good behavior he would be out in 13, he would be 73 years old. Cina was still beautiful and although she had lost everything, I knew there had to be men pursuing her. We were both getting older and for different reasons I too had few material possessions to show for my 50 plus years of existence. Back home opportunities for work still came my way, and after a western store bought most of my remaining buffalo, I started taking them. A courier job here and there, some light security work at Charlie's bar, but then in New York City while doing security for another major musical act I got my next money-making idea.

In Oklahoma and Texas people in the oil business had been making more money than they could spend, but a recent slump in price had them selling off their play toys. Boats, cars, and motor homes, even houses and land, were being sold at rock bottom prices. I noticed that in New York and all along the East coast where I'd been traveling lately these things were bringing top dollar. Upon returning to Oklahoma, still packing around the idea of making some money, I bought a motorhome cheap intending to sell it back East. With all my expenses I could see that I wouldn't make much just with the RV alone, but I still had two buffalo mounts left along with about 500 Mexican blankets and hoodies I'd traded for with a vendor. When I was last in Santa Fe I'd swapped him one of the buffalo heads. I'd sold a bunch of this stuff in Oklahoma before the market dried up and figured I could sell the rest along with the RV in New York.

The trip east went smoothly and I saved a lot of money staying in the motorhome. Once there, I found a location along a beachfront road I'd seen on a previous trip where other people set up and sold stuff. The Mexican blankets were a new thing many people had never seen before. The blankets and hoodies sold quickly but the buffalo heads were a different story. Although many people admired them, I would eventually sell them only by dropping my price to the point of breaking even again. When I sold out of blankets and buffalo, I listed the RV in a shoreline newspaper and with the price I asking, wasn't surprised with all the inquiries that came in. It sold the first week and I immediately started thinking about going back to Oklahoma to shop for another one. I had also found out during this last trip that outboard boat motors that had never been in salt water were in high demand on the East coast. A month later I was in Oklahoma buying another RV, several small outboard engines, and a few Western saddles I'd gotten my hands on that I thought I could sell.

What started as a trial run was becoming a regular thing as I would buy and sell half a dozen motor coaches, always filling them with other things I thought I could resell. It was on one of these trips that I met Gene Swaintek. Gene built both fancy homes along the coast and commercial buildings which was what he was working on the day we met. His company was building an addition to the existing town library in Guilford, Ct. and like many people in the area he liked to go to the town dock on his lunch hour. This was a scenic spot with beautiful views of the water that I frequently visited. Gene and I struck up a conversation when we both sat down at the same waterfront picnic table and by the time we had finished lunch he had offered me a job. He also had a place for me to park my motorhome and he was so shorthanded he didn't care if I worked a week or a month.

Within three weeks I had sold all my inventory and found a buyer for the motorhome which left me sleeping on a cot in Gene's shop building. After we finished up the library project I headed for Oklahoma where I already had another RV lined up. Gene was a good connection and from then on whenever I was in the area I always had a job and a place to stay.

Spending that much time on the road I also started writing about the many trips I'd taken and the things I'd seen. Never good at English in school, my scribblings were readable but rough. On one of these trips I had a chance encounter with a well-educated woman in Connecticut who read my material and encouraged me to write a column and send it in to my hometown paper in Bartlesville. During my next trip back to Oklahoma I contacted the publisher of the paper and reviewed my ideas. He liked the concept and I started the column the following week.

Whether writing about a nonprofit organization, a rodeo I was traveling to, a museum that caught my eye or just a famous person I was lucky enough to meet, all of these topics became part of my weekly column. At first writing a 600-word column was a challenge but over time it became easier and I found plenty of material to write about in my travels. Before it was sent off, my Connecticut coach would always correct and edit my writing.

In between selling RVs and working for Gene, when I was back in Oklahoma I occasionally took on other jobs. If a courier job took me to California, now I would write about the trip and anything along the way that got my attention. Whenever I was in a new town, museums were a favorite destination and I never had trouble finding stories to tell. From another delivery job I took hauling two high dollar horses from Oklahoma to a farm in Tennessee to a job in Alaska where an orphaned Delaware Indian girl hoped to find her real parents in Oklahoma I always found plenty to write about. Some jobs like finding the parents of the Delaware Indian girl took no time at all. Others took weeks, even months.

As age and old injuries began to catch up with me I began to avoid security jobs where muscle might be needed if I couldn't find some younger help. I had never saved a dime in my life so I needed to keep working and writing soon took on a larger role in my life.

Although I'd never written about the murder of E.C. Mullendore III I certainly knew about it. It had been the most sensational murder of the time. It caught my attention when the news came out about the capture of Damon "Chub" Anderson a man who law enforcement said was wanted for fleeing a 16 year-old pot conviction in Kansas. All the reports said he also had outstanding warrants in Oklahoma. This wasn't the so-called Damon Anderson from Seneca, Missouri, this was the real guy most people thought could solve the Mullendore shooting. Fortunately, I was in Bartlesville at the time and now that I was writing this weekly column there was no way I was going to miss his preliminary hearing.

Sheriff Frank Green had brought Chub back from Montana, where he'd been living the past 16 years, to his Sedan, Kansas, jail. Because of health issues after two days Chub had been transported to the county jail in Independence, Kansas which had better medical options for him.

I couldn't go anywhere in Oklahoma or Kansas where people weren't talking about the 1970 murder of E.C. Mullendore and Chub Anderson. It was consuming everyone I crossed paths with, and they all had a personal story to tell me either about the Mullendores' Cross Bell Ranch or Chub. I knew several people who had met Chub, a few of whom I felt probably knew him very well. Men he'd cowboyed with seemed to like him a lot; others called him a thief and a murderer. There were lots of women, past lovers and wannabes who had stories about how abusive and controlling he could be. Others said he was a fine man who got a bad rap.

At our first meeting which was held in a judge's chamber with Chub dressed in an inmate orange jumpsuit, handcuffed with guards on both sides, I had no idea I'd learn the secrets to his life. Our conversation was short, just a few words and then my phone number was passed to his lawyer. That was it. A call the next day from that same lawyer was followed by my second meeting with Chub at the Chautauqua County Courthouse in Sedan, Kansas, where he would be sentenced. A guilty plea to jumping bond on pot charges in Kansas from 1990 resulted in prison time, and as the deputies lead him out of the courthouse our second conversation was just about as brief as the first one. In the following weeks I received several phone calls from Chub who was now incarcerated in Lansing Correctional Facility. He arranged for me to visit on weekends and during our conversations I began thinking that this material could become a book. Chub was telling me about his youth and his parents, his brothers, and all those women I'd heard so much about.

We had been meeting for several weeks when I got a call from E.C. Mullendore's sister Katsy and her husband Jim Whittenberg. It would be the first of many calls as she wanted to know what, if anything, I was learning about her brother's death. After a meeting with Chub I would often fly to Dallas or Katsy would come to my house for a report. She made it plain she wanted all the details of her brother's murder and for everything to be kept quiet, at least for the time being which was fine with me.

Two months later she decided she wanted to talk to Chub herself, asking me to pass her wishes on to him and the warden which I did. Although the warden usually went out of his way to be helpful to me, in this instance he said that such a visit wouldn't happen, as crime victims are not allowed to meet with prisoners. When I conveyed his response to Katsy she was unfazed.

To my surprise two weeks later the warden granted Katsy's request even allowing her to bring a tape recorder, and the next time I saw her I heard the recording. At the beginning of their meeting she was very gracious and kind to Chub, asking if there was anything she could help him with. Then she got straight to the point. She wanted to know what had happened on the night of her brother's death and why he had been beaten and shot. Her voice broke as if she were crying but after a few minutes she regained her composure. She asked Chub if he was hiding something about someone who might have killed E.C. and why was he doing that?

Chub must have been sitting close to her as the volume on the recording never changed when he started to speak. He told Katsy a familiar story that she had always known was a lie.

"It was two men that jumped us and E.C. was already shot by the time I came downstairs. That's when I got shot myself but I chased them. I killed them both and buried the bodies in a pond dam out on the ranch."

Chub continued with a few more details but Katsy said very little in response.

I had been listening quietly to the tape with my head down and when I looked up Katsy was wiping tears from her eyes.

"I want you to keep us informed, said Jim. I'll pay you but keep Katsy and me up to date."

Katsy and Jim had lots of lawyer and Katsy had told me she was consulting them regularly about Chub as well as our meetings.

I was right in the middle of the most famous unsolved murder in the southwest and I began to include tidbits about the case in my weekly column while I continued working with Chub putting his life story together. During our visits I would bring up something I had researched like a relationship with a woman or a robbery he had committed or his pot growing. We'd visit about it and I'd document everything he said, then I would try to find some kind of proof that what he had told me was true. Sometimes I discovered that he was feeding me a line of bullshit with some stories but others turned out to be true.

We had established a good relationship and shortly before his release from prison Chub called to say that his ex-brother-in-law Lonnie Brown would be picking him up and he would call me as soon as he could. I called his cousin Ike immediately because I knew he had been worried about where Chub would stay and the relief in his voice was obvious. Ike was the only family member who had visited Chub at the prison and who was really trying to help him, despite his misgivings about his past behavior. From our first meeting it was obvious that Ike's morals were the complete opposite of his first cousin's but they had been close as kids and he still cared about him.

We were happy that Lonnie had gotten involved even though the pick-up was kind of secretly arranged by him at the last minute, which both Ike and I felt was strange.

A few days later Chub called, telling me where he was and giving me a brief description of how his release had gone. After spending a summer with no air conditioning in a prison built when President Lincoln was in office, he was thrilled to be out. However, Lansing had been both good and bad.

He had been locked up in a small cell but his health had improved there and he believed his 16 years of being a wanted man were behind him now.

BEFORE THE DEW

Not Much Time Left

Chub wasn't free yet. There were probation officer meetings and the law in Oklahoma still had warrants out for him but he still wanted to talk with me. We met sometimes twice a day and if I was traveling on another story for my weekly column or had some kind of out of town job, we would talk on the phone. Few other people came to see him and in a strange way I felt sorry for him. Here he was so famous without much longer to live but no one came to visit. I wondered aloud to him about it but he said he didn't care. He did like hearing about my travels and all the stuff I got into. We would talk about the Mullendore murder and what he knew but I never pushed him. If he wanted to tell me something, I let him. He was the only one that knew what had happened that night, now that he was out of prison I was hoping he would speak more freely.

Chub was a sick man and was having kidney dialysis every other day. I knew he wouldn't last long and he did too. A year or two at most was what everyone had told me but so far, he had proved them wrong. It had now been three years since his capture when my involvement with him started. His life story was about done when he moved into a nursing home. He had moved from his place in Niotze, Kansas to Caney, Kansas and this would be his last stop. By then I had learned the whole story of the tragic end of E.C.'s life but I couldn't let go, I had to stay with Chub until the end.

I seldom went a day without visiting him and as always, I recorded everything we talked about. His cousin Ike and Chub's best friend from grade school Charles Blevins had done a lot to encourage him to keep working with me because it seemed to give him a sense of purpose.

I often read parts of the book to Chub and kept him up to date through all the rewrites and changes to the manuscript which was now around 500 pages long. I also explained to him that it would take a long time to get the book in print and it would also be expensive. Counting printing, some advertising, a lawyer and a few other things, I was looking at $45,000 and change. I'd already spent that and more developing the book. I told him there was no way I had either that much cash on hand or credit at the bank. I'd been on the project for close to four years already and yes everyone knew this was a story that needed to be told, but how was I going to get the financing I needed? I hashed this problem over for several weeks.

I'd hung out with folks that had money in my life and to them, the ones with real money, $45,000 wasn't anything. My first thought was to form a partnership where each man or woman would put up $5,000.00 to receive a share, and that way if the book was a flop, which was a possibility, no one would really be out much. A couple of the guys I was thinking about asking to get involved I knew from my basketball days at the local YMCA. These were people I'd known for a long time and I was sure they would be on board as soon as I gave them the details. The first one I figured would set the tempo but I didn't have a lot of time. I was afraid Chub would die before I got the book published and I didn't want that to happen.

Although the manuscript was basically finished, I was still doing a lot of research on Chub. I was also traveling for my weekly column and selling everything I could do without just to keep the project going. This first guy couldn't say No, I thought. What was $5,000 when he had a chance to make history in solving the Mullendore murder and as an added bonus, getting his name included in the book? We had played many a game of noon hour basketball together and he was a prominent leader in the community, giving generously of both his time and money to many non-profit organizations.

I sensed Roger's reaction as soon as he said he'd think about it and to make me feel even worse, I had to call him a couple of weeks later to get his response. He told me things were tight and he didn't have the money. It brought me down and I received the same answer from Bob, the second man on my list who was also quite well to do. He said there were too many loose ends and with that I just gave up on my plan.

I told Chub about my disappointment but he just laughed. Although he didn't personally know these friends of mine, he knew people he would say. Disappointment meant nothing to him. I found he didn't have that feeling in his psychological makeup and I was finding there were a lot of other feelings that didn't register in his thinking either. I was putting his reactions in the story I was writing about him but that didn't help my disappointment or the money I needed to get the book published. Despite the deaths I had experienced and occasional financial problems I had never been much of drinker. But now the frustration I felt about getting our project into print weighed on me and I began drinking, first just one cocktail a night, then two. I was almost to the end of my line as the fishermen say, and so was Chub's health. One day during my visit it looked like he was taking his last breath as he smiled telling me not to give up.

That was encouraging. Here I had written every piece of dirt on the guy you could imagine. I'd written what he'd told me and solved the most famous murder in the whole Southwest, pointing the finger right at him and he was telling me not to give up. So, how could I?

I was raised up from the bottom that day and returning home I heard some more good news when a man who read my column called me. His name was Jerry Stover and he lived in Stillwater, Oklahoma. A retired railroad man, Jerry had been reading my column for years and asked if there was any way he could get involved with me in putting Chub's life story together. After Chub's comments, Jerry was the second good thing to happen to me in one day, and when I mentioned a partnership, he jumped right on board. Unbelievably, the next day a distant relative called with basically the same story. Although Mike Kelly was living out of state, he read the column on the internet and like Jerry wanted to be involved. This would be the last day I needed a drink to go on and I put that chapter in my life behind me forever.

The project gained more momentum when I talked to Elise, another reader who I had recently met from Tulsa. It would be my readers who would keep the project upright but the big money for publishing a book was still far off. My new partners were giving me ideas for the project and through some research I discovered Kickstarter, a fundraising concept that was just starting up at the time. From what everyone was telling me it might be a promising way to raise money for the publishing costs. There would be about $5,000.00 in upfront costs for the technical end of things and graphic design. so, I hired a company called Bit Brilliant to help.

To me this Kickstarter thing looked like good publicity. They were advertising all over the world so even if I didn't raise the funds, the exposure would be worth something. As it turned out, that was about all I got out of it. The way Kickstarter works you just have a short window of time to raise the money and if you do not meet your goal you don't receive any funds. The whole project fell apart right in the middle of the campaign when BitBrilliant folded, leaving me without technical support.

Either by faith, which I think it was, or luck, during our next phone call Katsy asked if she could help out with some of my expenses, an offer Jim had made in our first meeting some four years earlier. I had turned him down then not wanting to seem like their spy. I told Jim that but he said that's not what he or Katsy wanted. They were still a bit scared of Chub's reputation and she only wanted to know what had happened to her brother promising not to prosecute Chub. Katsy told me this on more than one occasion and this time I decided to accept their offer for support. Nothing else would be said and she asked for nothing in exchange except for me to tell her if I thought Chub would talk or if he turned violent toward her family.

For three months I received a small check from her; no note or request, just a check. Chub's health was so bad I couldn't see that he presented any kind of danger to anyone and I felt kind of guilty about taking her money but she insisted. Her daddy had told her it was Chub all along and that E.C. wouldn't have shot anybody. She had spent forty years with this on her mind, grieving for her brother. She wanted to hear Chub admitting it all and saying that E.C. hadn't shot him. She also believed his ex-brother-in-law Lonnie Brown might have had something to do with the murder.

I felt compelled to help her before Chub died and I came up with a plan. I told Katsy I thought Chub would tell her what had happened if I offered him money. I didn't know how much he would want or if this would even work so she just gave me $10,000. I met Chub at the Caney Kitchen but when I told him about the cash and what Katsy wanted he said he'd have to think it over. Then it was too late. Chub died a few weeks later without ever giving me an answer and I returned the money to Katsy but I still had work to do.

During the time I'd known Chub I'd met many people through my weekly column, both famous and infamous. I'd covered several trials that had caught the public's attention, many times hoping to get a bite from a national reporter on the book. Now a year after his death that's what led me to Boston.

On June 22, 2011, a man named James Whitely Bulger was captured in an apartment in Santa Monica, California. By coincidence I had been in California to meet with film producer Wyatt McCray who lived just up the coast from where Bulger was captured. I'd just sent a story to my editor back home when she told me of his capture. Bulger had been indicted by federal prosecutors in Boston and all the TV news channels were carrying the breaking story of this big-time organized crime boss who had been on the run for 16 years. I went to the apartment where he had been captured and then wrote all about it in my next week's column including a detailed description of his criminal record. Bulger faced nineteen murder charges along with conspiracy to commit murder, extortion, narcotics and money laundering. Throw in a crooked FBI agent and a brother who was president of the Massachusetts Senate and who was also believed to have aided his brother, it was no wonder dozens of reporters were covering the story. This was the opportunity I'd been looking for and I wanted to be right in the middle of things.

I had a close friend I could stay with who lived close to Boston by train which would take me to the downtown area. Eight blocks away on Boston Harbor sat the John Joseph Moakly United States Courthouse where the trial would be held. Thank goodness for a beautiful setting as I would wait each morning for hours with the other reporters who were there. Whitey was always taken to the back of the building through a guarded door but the witnesses and jurors came in through the front where all the reporters stood. The families of the murder victims and the witnesses were fair game for the media who were looking for quotes but that's not what I was after. I was making contacts in the media that would hopefully come in handy later in marketing my book. The trail lasted three months which passed quickly. I was on a first name basis with some of these folks by the time the jury found Bulger guilty of murder and a dozen other felony counts. He was sentenced to two consecutive life sentences plus five years and during the sentencing process I got a break. Whitey had two brothers, William Bulger who was a big-shot in the Massachusetts State Senate who never came to the trial and another brother who always there but shunned the press. One day out of the blue he started a conversation with me in an elevator and as we walked out into the swarm of waiting journalists he shook my hand and said "see you tomorrow."

After that we spoke on several occasions, not talking about anything in particular and never mentioning his brother or the trial. Other reporters who had tried to get an interview with him and failed noticed our meetings and before long they were inquiring as to just what this brother of Whitey's who never talked was telling me. Although he never told me anything of consequence, as the result of our conversation I made the kind of press contact I had been hoping for.

At the top of my contact list was Rikki Kleinman a well-established lawyer, crime reporter and CBS commentator who was also married to the Police Commissioner in New Yok City, Bill Bratton. She was a published author and once I got the opportunity to tell her about my book she was more than willing to give me suggestions.

After the Bulger trial ended I went back to Oklahoma and worked through many rewrites of Chub's story. Then another trial that wasn't far from home got the nation's attention. The shooting deaths of well-known marine sniper Chris Kyle and his friend Chad Littlefield made national news. When I heard that several of the media people I'd met at Whitey Bolger's trial were going to cover the proceedings in Stephenville, Texas, I thought it would be another opportunity for some free publicity about the book, something I desperately needed.

I spent three weeks at the trial researching the shooter Eddie Ray Routh for my readers and exploring the "whys" and "how comes" of this tragic story. The media coverage was even more intense here than it had been in Boston and I made several new important contacts. Trial after trial, wherever I went I told my own tale of murder.

BEFORE THE DEW

Another Great Man

Whenever I could I'd head for a place I found especially inspirational to write. All my life I'd loved Will Rogers and read all I could about him. I found his friend Waite Phillips just as interesting.

Waite was a millionaire philanthropist who donated thousands of acres of land just outside of Cimarron, New Mexico to the boy scouts in the 1950s. He also gave them millions of dollars to maintain the property in perpetuity.
I was never a scout myself nor was Waite but I found his story so compelling that I've never been able to forget it and in Cimarron, I'd find the will and the way to go forward.

My love of Philmont Boy Scout Ranch and Cimarron as well as the fact that it was a short 12-hour drive from home brought me back to the area several times a year. Chub too had liked the area and had taken one of his wives skiing at the Angel Fire Ski Resort which lies about 30 miles west of Cimarron.

The old Santa Fe cattle trail of the 1800s ran right through Cimarron and four miles south was where Waite had built his ranch The UUBar. This was his favorite place in the world and just down the road sits the historic Saint James Hotel.

Originally built by Henri Lambert in 1872, it had been the only place to stay along the cattle trail and the history of the hotel had always been a great source of material for my column. Billy the Kid, Buffalo Bill, the Earp brothers, the list of the good guys and bad guys who had stayed there was endless. Over those early years there had been 27 men killed there and dozens of other shootings. It had the kind of history I loved, but the Saint James had fallen on hard times. It had been up for sale for a couple of years and I had followed the situation hoping for some kind of angel to come flying in and save it. The town of Cimarron is out of the way for most people who are not involved in scouting, fishing, or winter snow skiing and for years it had been struggling as well.

Was it research for the book or just an excuse to run out to the area? Whatever it was, this trip would change the whole development of the book.

I had been so tied up with Chub and the rewriting that two years had slipped by since my last visit to the area and what I found when I returned was unbelievable. What had been a rundown structure with a leaky roof had been converted into something close to a museum. I had seen old photographs of the hotel and the exterior had been repainted to match the original color. The inside was decorated to look just like it had when Lambert opened the place. Furniture from that era filled every room along with photographs of all the famous people who had stayed there. Buffalo, elk, and mountain lion mounts filled every space. The bar stools, chairs and tables, all original pieces, were also in the same spots shown in the old photographs. It was amazing to me that the place was even open and now it was running and plum full of people.

The changes in the restaurant were as unbelievable as the changes in the building. Someone had to be driving to Santa Fe if not daily then every other day for the ingredients to make the fresh dishes they were offering. I asked my waitress, a local girl who was filling me in on all the new developments at the hotel, about the extraordinary menu. She told me the cook was not your ordinary cook but the former executive chef for Oklahoma Governor Frank Keating. For eight years this guy had cooked for everyone from presidents to movie stars in the governor's mansion, and I couldn't believe he was here in the little town of Cimarron. What was he doing way out in the middle of New Mexico? And who had bought this famous old hotel spending, from what I could see, a couple million dollars remodeling and furnishing it then bringing in this high-dollar chef? The waitress told me that the new owner was also remodeling several other pieces of property he owned in the area. It was becoming obvious that this fellow was employing every able-bodied person in the town who wanted a job.

An angel had come to Cimarron, New Mexico all right and I got another surprise when I learned that he was from Oklahoma. Bob Funk was as well known in Oklahoma City for his philanthropic work as he was for his business ventures and the more I found out about him the more I liked him. A family man devoted to God and country, he'd come from poor folks and through luck he would say and hard work had created a company that brought in several billion dollars a year finding jobs for people. Past President of the Federal Reserve board in Kansas City, owner of several professional sports franchises, and one of the largest land owners in the country, Bob Funk was an important guy. He had money, the kind of money to put into an old hotel like the Saint James, not to make money but to save history. The next week I wrote a story about his preservation of the historic hotel and added that I wondered what kind of man this Bob Funk must be to do this, adding that I'd like to meet him someday.

Express Employment Professionals is a big company with over 800 offices located in several countries with thousands of employees. I mailed a copy of the article to the corporate office in Oklahoma City but after that I didn't think much more about it. What would be the chance a man of his stature, obviously busy, would read my little column and decide to call me yet I just had a premonition that something was going to happen. That premonition came true when none other than Bob Funk himself called me.

His personal secretary Carol Lane had passed my column on to him and he wanted to thank me personally for what I had written. From the first few words he spoke it was obvious that

Bob could communicate with anybody; rich, poor, educated or not. He had a way of engaging people with a truly caring spirit. That first 10-minute phone call was followed by another call from Carol to set up an appointment with Bob a few days later. I used the time to do some more research about the man.

Born to a Christian family on a dairy farm in Washington State he'd been poor, real poor. He'd been quoted often throughout his adult life that it had always been his loving family's upbringing and Christian principles along with hard work that had made him successful. Now in his early seventies, it appeared to me he had plenty of everything except ego. From everything I was reading, he ran his company not with a strong arm but with compassion and it was plain he wasn't an ordinary fellow. In fact, I was surprised he even had the time to see me. At our meeting, instead of me interviewing him, he wanted to hear all about my life's travels, where I was from and what I'd been doing. Of course, I told him all about meeting Chub and writing a book about the Mullendore murder.

Walking out of his office an hour later, he asked me to arrange another appointment through Carol saying he looked forward to seeing me again. In the hallway several coat-and-tie guys were waiting their turn to see him. They all greeted me with a smile and a handshake, probably thinking I was somebody special since I'd been in his office for so long. Why we got along so well I don't know. I was just being me and I think Bob was just being Bob. It felt like I'd known the guy for years and we were best friends. I sat in my car in the huge parking lot of his office building for a good 30 minutes thinking about it, amazed that a guy who was so successful, a guy with so many newspaper stories, even books, written about him had taken a liking to me.

After writing my weekly column for close to 10 years, I'd had the opportunity to spend time with many fascinating people but Bob Funk was a different type of man.

I could see he was making decisions every day involving millions of dollars and affecting thousands of lives. His wisdom and advice were turning out to be more valuable than money to me. It boosted my confidence knowing Bob had faith in the future success of my project.

As it turned out I would need all the advice and encouragement I could get because two weeks later I was subpoenaed to appear before a multi-county Grand Jury which wanted to question me about the book and E.C.'s murder. My bank account had just a few hundred dollars in, there was no way I could afford a lawyer so I'd have to go it alone. On the day of my deposition, twelve jurors and a handful of alternates listened as the Attorney General and the Osage County D.A. questioned me. I told them that in his own words Chub said he had shot E.C. and enlisted his brother-in-law's help to create an alibi. No detail was left out, it was a straight-out confession and I had it all on tape.

The Attorney General wanted the tapes too and by the time the hearing was over I had been placed under a gag order which meant no future book sales.

Experienced writers and publishers say to expect hardships if you want to be a writer. Well, I'd faced difficulties throughout the project and the gag order was just the most recent. I'd spent too much time and money on the book to quit now and as things happened the solution came out of the blue during lunch with an old friend of mine.

I'd met Mike Smith right after Don died when he was a young boy of ten or eleven. He and his family lived next door to a house I was working on during my early days in construction. We had stayed in touch and he had occasionally traveled with me when he wasn't in school. We were having lunch together and talking about his sister Ree Drummond who had become so successful when the thought hit me that their cousin who was a lawyer might be able to help me. I'd only met Gentner

Drummond briefly but I'd gotten a good feeling from him at the time. A member of the prominent Drummond family from Osage County, he was a rancher, lawyer, and like Bob a big philanthropist.

The day after my lunch with Mike I decided to drive to Tulsa and see if I could meet with him. Although I turned up at his office unexpectedly, he found time to talk to me. During our meeting I explained the situation to him and he offered to have one of his attorneys work with me on a pro bono basis! My next meeting with another attorney at the firm, Harvey Grauberger, resulted in a formal letter addressed to the State Attorney General asking for the gag order to be lifted immediately. Gentner and Harvey both thought the letter would be sufficient but before I mailed it I asked Bob Funk's personal attorney Kent Gardner to review it was well. By this point in our relationship Bob had offered Kent's services to me whenever I needed them and I'd taken him up on his offer several times. After making a few suggestions, he too felt the letter would do the trick. The three attorneys were right and within a few weeks I received notice that the gag order was lifted, allowing me to go forward with the book.

I still stayed in touch with all the people I had met while I was putting Chub's story together, from his cousin Ike who still told me my visits had been the only thing that had kept Chub going to the director of the nursing home who had always encouraged me. Chub and I had formed a bond while we worked so closely on his life story but I saw his good and bad sides clearly. He was not a hero to me in the way of Will Rogers, Waite Phillips, or even my new friend Bob Funk. Strangely, after all the time we spent together I didn't mourn when he died. I just became more determined to publish his story.

Through Bob I'd recently met a couple of film producers who were on the board of the Western Heritage and Cowboy Hall of Fame in Oklahoma City, which he was president of.

Bob had arranged a dinner with the producers and after they read the manuscript they had several recommendations for my project. The most important one was to have an entertainment lawyer review my work. They pointed me to attorney J. Shanker whose offices were out in California. After I consulted with him he suggested a writing coach he knew in Florida.

I'd known all along I needed a bit more direction in my writing of the book from day one. I was a newspaper columnist and without the help of my lady friend on the Long Island Sound I wouldn't have gotten that far. It didn't surprise me that I needed help in my writing but the cost would. I had invested in a six-acre piece of property several years before outside the town of Bartlesville. The land was the last thing I had, but now that would have to be sold.

BEFORE THE DEW

Good Guys and Bad Guys

Daniel Roth had a successful career as a writing coach and in earlier years had been a successful writer himself. After a lengthy phone call during which I explained who I was and that Jay had referred me, we got down to business. I told him about Chub, E.C.'s murder, the 300,000-acre ranch along with the family owning the New Orleans Saints football team. I also mentioned that E.C. held the largest life insurance policy ever written on an individual anywhere in the world at the time of the murder. I had his attention and he also had mine when he said his price just for looking at my work was $5,000.00. After that he'd let me know how much more his services would be, depending on how rough it was. I swallowed hard and wrote him a check.

I mailed the manuscript and then I didn't hear from Daniel for three weeks. When he finally got back to me he said I had a great story and he couldn't put it down, commenting that my writing skills were also good. He thought the story needed editing but his main concern was the lack of a narrator. Who was telling the story of Chub and E.C. getting killed? It took another reread on my part along with a couple thousand dollars in advice from Daniel before I got it but when I did it was like turning on a light switch. The narrator of this book had to be either E.C.'s sister Katsy or me. The most gracious lady I had ever met, I'd been keeping Katsy in the loop about the progress of the book all along and I didn't think she would want that level of involvement. After meeting with her and explaining Daniel's suggestions we both agreed I needed to be the narrator. Katsy was in her late 70s now and her husband Jim in his late 80s and they were enjoying life to the fullest.

She had little interest in being tied to a desk but I would hear from her on occasion when things about the murder would pop up in her memory.

Rereads followed by adjustments along with editing work it seemed it was all never ending. One particular piece I edited out was the story of the Dixie Mafia gang. Chub had hung out with gang member Albert MacDonald and I found plenty of material about the gang during my research.

Their association along with the life story of another gang member, the Queen of the Tulsa bootleggers Cleo Epps, had captured my attention but Daniel pointed out that these characters did not play a role in E.C.'s murder. The Dixie Mafia was a loosely run group of criminals who were in and out of McAlester during the time Chub was there. The group included Tom Lester Pugh, Garland Rex Brinlee, Jr., Albert McDonald and Cleo Epps who was McDonald's girlfriend at the time. Although everyone in the gang was older than Chub, he had some contact with all of them in his younger years before the murder.

Tom Lester Pugh was one the most notorious crime figures Chub would meet at McAlester. Pugh had received a life term for the murder of Arles Delbert Self who disappeared just as he was about to testify against Pugh and Albert McDonald during a grand jury investigation into the bombing of District Judge Fred Nelson's car which occurred while the judge was in it. Pugh would also be charged with the murder Cleo Epps who had been called as a witness against the gang. In addition to these crimes, Pugh was convicted of the armed robbery and kidnapping of Joseph LaFortune, Sr., the father of former Tulsa Mayor Bill LaFortune. This conviction drew a 25 to 30-year prison term so Pugh had little hope of parole. Eventually Pugh was transferred to a federal prison in Kentucky and after this transfer he was convicted of masterminding an inmate drug ring that sold millions of dollars of illegal drugs throughout the prison systems in California, Arizona, Kentucky, Missouri and Oklahoma. When he was discovered plotting from prison the murder of two judges in Arizona Pugh managed to escape for a short time but was recaptured in Irving, Texas after committing 17 robberies.

At the time he was arrested Pugh was planning to kill another law enforcement officer, Tulsa District Attorney S.M. Buddy Fallis. Convictions for murder, armed robbery, kidnapping and bootlegging led to a life sentence plus 10-year term for Pugh.

Chub told me he had also crossed paths with Pugh's partner Garland Rex Brinlee, Jr., another member of the Dixie Mafia who had been in and out of jail most of his life. When Bristow school teacher Fern Bolding was blown up as she started the family pick-up a few days before her husband Donald was schedule to testify against Brinlee on stolen vehicle charges, the cops immediately suspected him and Pugh.

The old newspaper coverage about the case said that Brinlee was a plumber and nightclub owner in Tahlequah who had a history of violence. He had bragged to several people about putting dynamite under Bolding's car and had sent threatening letters to both Governor David Hall and Tulsa attorney Pat Williams, one of Chub's future lawyers. The letters stated that he "owed" them four sticks of dynamite and intended to pay them back for the wrongs they had committed against him. Hall had signed an extradition request that brought Brinlee back to Oklahoma from a Missouri prison and Williams had represented Brinlee's ex-wife during their divorce trial. Attorney Thomas Dee Frasier who defended Brinlee in the Bolding case (and lost) and Robert Meder, a state senator and bank officer who had foreclosed on Brinlee's apartment building in Tahlequah to satisfy a $50,000 legal fee for Frasier were also threatened with the gang's favorite method of removing obstacles: dynamite!

Apparently, Brinlee's calm demeanor could erupt into violent rage as KTUL-TV photographer Richard Wilson discovered at a hearing in Okmulgee where Brinlee viscously attacked him in the courtroom. When Brinlee was returned to the Tulsa County jail, the photographer for the Tulsa World, Don Hamilton was there and decided it was better for his health to keep his distance after snapping a photo of the prisoner. Over time Rex Brinlee became widely regarded as the most dangerous man in the Oklahoma prison system.

Chub knew some of these characters in Oklahoma's outlaw past but not all of them. He had met Cleo Epps who was one of the most interesting to me. Cleo started her adult life as a school teacher but the lure of big money drew her into the illegal booze market in Oklahoma. This path led her to the Dixie Mafia and then finally to the bottom of a septic tank in west Tulsa.

Cleo was born in a rural area of Fort Smith, Arkansas as Cleo Gilbert. She went to college and then moved to Stony Point, Oklahoma where she taught in a one room school.

She became an admired member of the community because of her commitment to her school and folks remembered how she pushed her students to do their best with love and understanding.

An early first marriage to a heavy drinker did not last long and her second marriage ended quickly as well but it was a turning point in her life. Cleo's second husband was involved in the bootlegging business in Oklahoma which at the time was a dry state. Although she was not a drinker herself, she could see the money that was there to be made. After their divorce she stayed in the business, moving to Tulsa.

Cleo had frequent run-ins with the law but by all accounts, they were mostly cordial. She supplied liquor to many of Tulsa's leading citizens as well as to most of the big hotels in town and she considered herself to be on friendly terms with both lawmakers and law breakers. Through her bootlegging business she met Dixie Mafia enforcer Albert McDonald whom she fell madly in love with. Like the other gang members McDonald preferred dynamite to bullets but in a pinch bullets would work too. As Cleo would later find out, he was a man without a conscience or any concern for his victims. I was intrigued by the gang members and thought it revealed something about Chub that he had been on friendly terms with them, but ultimately that was not enough to keep their stories in the book.

After eight years I had written ninety-thousand words and I was ready for a professional proofreader for one last review looking for misspellings and typos. I was unfamiliar with the process and didn't realize it would lead to another reread on my part and then another three months of adjustments before the manuscript was ready for a graphic designer to do the layout. I'd selected Johnny King in Tulsa because I was familiar with his work for the Nature Conservancy, an organization I'd written about several times.

I'd chosen Southwestern Printing in Oklahoma City because they had an excellent reputation for quality and had given me several options for the format of the book. But before I sent the manuscript to the printer Katsy and Jim wanted to look it over one more time so I sent them two copies. Two weeks later to the day she called and with her husband Jim on the speakerphone began to cry telling me how much it meant to her knowing who had killed E.C. We had a long conversation and Katsy asked me a lot of questions about the funding for the project. My expenses to date totaled close to $100,000.00 which included travel, legal advice, graphic design and printing costs as well as my work with Daniel Roth. Now I was getting ready to spend another $45,000.00 for the printing all adding up to close to $150,000.00. I couldn't believe it again when Jim offered to repay me for my efforts. Katsy followed up Jim's offer telling me the story would probably never be printed. Jim also mentioned I'd have to sign some confidentiality agreements meaning I could never talk about it as well. I held my breath when I told them I'd have to think about it. $150,000.00! I could pay back everyone who had had faith in me but I'd put in a lot of time and effort and I wasn't sure what to do when it hit me. Bob Funk was the only man I knew who I felt could advise me and I called his office right away hoping he wasn't traveling. Carol had recently retired and his new assistant Dana Miller scheduled an appointment for the next day. I knew Bob went to work early and the next morning I was there waiting. When I told him Katsy and Jim wanted to buy the manuscript he immediately rejected the idea. He said this book could be worth much more to me in the long run and what about all the people waiting to hear the true story of E.C.'s murder? I'd been thinking the same thing since Katsy and Jim's offer. This story wasn't just a book it was meant to be movie. I'd known all along I couldn't let go of it and I was relieved that Katsy wasn't angry when I called and told her.

Still Alive

Twenty-five hundred hard backed books would fill three pallets, each five feet tall. This was a lot of books and a big gamble for me. My first book would be given to Bob Funk the guy who had inspired me to go on. We were meeting about once a month but more importantly, he began inviting me to big events which gave me the opportunity to promote the book in a wider circle of contacts. The second and third books were sent to CBS correspondents Rikki Kleiman and Mark Strassmann. After meeting at the Whitey Bulger trial Rikki and I had gotten together a few times for breakfast in New York City where she lived. A regular legal analyst for CBS This Morning she had been interested in E.C.'s murder since our first visit and asked me to send her a book as soon as they were available.

Mark Strassmann was another big-time CBS correspondent who had been at the trial of the man who killed American Sniper Chris Kyle and his friend Tad Littlefield. Like Rikki, Mark covered news stories around the world. When we met in Stephenville, Texas during the trial he too felt I was on to a great story and wanted one of the first books. I wound up sending out over a hundred free books not only to reporters I'd met but anyone I thought could give me some free publicity, all the time not knowing if I'd written something anyone would read. I was also curious as to how the people mentioned in the book would take it.

The official book release date by coincidence was on the anniversary of E.C.'s murder, September 26, 2015, forty-five years later. It would be held during the annual Tom Mix Days and Dewey Wild West Celebration. City leaders had asked if I could come to the event months in advance hoping the release of my book would draw a crowd. The two-day celebration is usually well attended and as the 26th drew near my personal security became an issue. I had received anonymous death threats in the mail along with strange phone calls before the book's release and the threats increased after word of its publication spread. I wasn't overly worried but with all the people in town the organizers were concerned. Some of the people who had known Chub were convinced he was blameless and didn't want his image tarnished by my book.

Any friend of Chub's made the organizers nervous so when September 26th arrived two plain-clothes security officers were on hand to make sure I was safe. Seeing the line of people wrapped around the block I was glad they were there. Still, I was more worried that the book might not be worth reading than that I might be shot by an old friend of Chub's.

The historic Dewey Hotel hadn't seen a crowd like this since the heyday of the rodeo in the 1930s. Men and women, young and old, everyone wanted to know who had killed E.C. and what Chub had told me about it. Even Chub's brother would stand in line and pick up several books as did Lonnie Brown's grandson. There was no trouble that day and the book signing was followed by another one the next day at Prairie Song, a replica of an old western town created and built by Marilyn Tate and her husband Kenneth. It was all part of a celebration that had been going on for years. I would wind up selling or giving away half of the 2,500 books during the first couple of weeks I had them and more importantly people like it. The book was a local success and positive reviews poured in. but there were a few problems. My proofreader who had come so highly recommended had missed a lot of punctuation errors, typos, and misspellings that were being brought to my attention by readers. Before I ordered another round of books I wanted these mistakes corrected which meant finding a new proofreader and reading through it again before sending the changes to Southwestern. The printing process alone takes a month or more so give or take a few days I was looking at maybe two months before delivery of the next shipment. I'd be out of books by then if sales continued the way they were going but my other problem was I still had half of the first order on hand. I would need to come up with another large deposit for the second printing. The way things were going I could have been making more money working at a grocery store.

I needed to order those books and when Southwestern agreed to finance half of the future shipment I could handle the rest of the costs but I also had to find a new proofreader. I found the person I needed right under my nose when my editor at the Bartlesville Examiner Enterprise mentioned she was looking for some extra work. I'd admired her writing skills for years and soon Susan was reading the first copy of the book. While Susan and the staff at Southwestern were working on revisions to the manuscript, I was traveling to every place where I thought I could sell a few books. Gun shows would become my favorite sales venue but I also went to boat and travel shows. It seemed three out of every four people at these shows had heard of E.C.'s murder. One weekend I would be in Kansas City, the next a town in Arkansas or Texas and then back to Oklahoma. My challenge was how to break out of the region with a story that I now knew people enjoyed reading about even if they had never heard of the murder. Some of the communities I visited had unsolved murders of their own but none of them involved 300,000-acre ranches, huge life insurance policies or a suspect who went on the run and lived under an alias for sixteen years. Everyone I talked to told me it was made for a motion picture. Sometimes I got to where I was just nodding in agreement I heard it so many times.

The new shipment of books came in just as college football season started and hoping to capitalize on E.C. having been a college student at the University of Oklahoma I started doing a few book signings during games on what's called Campus Corner. This area is a six-block gathering place of shops and bars and on game days the streets are closed while thousands of OU fans make their way to the game. Balfour is a memorabilia store that has been in business in the same place for 42 years. They sell everything from t shirts, glasses and plates to umbrellas-all with the OU emblem on them. The store was also once owned by one of E. C's fraternity brothers, Grover Ozmun. The current owner Jerry Hatter bought Balfour from Grover 12 years ago. When I approached him about selling my book in his store, Jerry had never heard of E.C. or the murder. But after calling Grover and finding out how big a deal it was back in 1970 he agreed to let me set up during OU's first home game. Close to 90,000 fans had come to watch the start of what looked like a promising season for the Oklahoma team. The Sooners had an experienced quarterback in Baker Mayfield who many were already calling a Heisman Trophy shoe in. The team also had three NFL type receivers, a solid defense, and a coach whom whenever he decided to retire was expected to go straight into the college football hall of fame. With all the hype going on about the team and the first game I expected a big crowd on Campus Corner and I was right.

Balfour sits right in the middle of Campus Corner and for years during pregame celebrations Jerry has had a live radio show going on before and after games right in his store. Past and present day football players come and go while out front the OU marching band plays. Dozens of street vendors who sell everything from balloons and cotton candy to OU game day tickets line the streets. For parking close to the stadium if you get there early property owners charge $25.00 a spot and the farther you get away the cheaper it gets. Being as it was my first game and I was unfamiliar with everything that was about to happen I parked five blocks away paid $10 and walked, carrying my books. I'd planned to get to Balfour early so I could see the live radio show. Jerry had mentioned I could come and go and stay as long as I wanted. He also said he had a friend who wanted to talk to me. It was Grover Ozmun and he was waiting when I got to Balfour. Grover had known E.C. in college and was anxious to visit with me about him.

I had talked to several of E.C.'s friends back in Bartlesville during my research for the book and most said E.C. had gotten a bad rap in the press. For over 40 years E.C. had been run down for many different things including his business practices and personal life but his friends who had truly known him said these things were just not true. I had wanted to put that in my book but had promised Katsy that I would leave E.C.'s personal life out of Chub's story. Now here was another friend telling me what a good person E.C. had been and how generous he had been with his money. Grover and I had a good hour-long conversation and afterward he gave me E.C.'s fraternity photograph and the phone numbers of other college friends who would verify that everything he had told me was true. Settling in to get ready for the radio show, I kept thinking that it wasn't right not to have said more about E.C. and how his friends had felt about him in the book. It had been his sister's call and I couldn't change it now that the book was in print but still it just didn't seem fair.

BEFORE THE DEW

New York City or Bust

The host of the radio program was the great OU All-American and professional football player Teddy Lehman. Teddy's guest that day was a man many in the OU world believe was the greatest runner in OU history, Joe Washington. Little Joe as he became known, had come from Port Arthur, Texas to play football for the University of Oklahoma Sooners and play he did. Small in size but big in heart, starting in 1972 he made every all-American team in the country. He finished up his college career with 4071 rushing yards and thirty-nine touchdowns.

Coach Barry Switzer was quoted as saying that Joe would have doubled those numbers if he had kept him in throughout the games. The Sooners were usually so far ahead at halftime that he would take Joe out. A first-round draft pick in 1976, Joe went on to become a premier running back and earned a Super bowl ring with the Washington Redskins in 1982.

Joe had just put out a book about his career and after the show he hung around autographing and selling the book right next to me. We sat side-by-side for two hours Joe autographing his book and me mine. At the next Saturday game, we did it again and then again at the following game. We were becoming friends and after he read my book he started calling me Chub in jest. We would meet up at Balfour the Friday before every game to autograph books and sometimes for lunch. Joe was also the head man of Varsity O, which is an organization led by the University for all past letterman in any sport, male or female if you lettered you are a member. It's a big group that numbers in the hundreds that meet for their own tailgate party right across from the stadium before every home game and Joe was in charge of it, always inviting me to join them.

I was passing out hundreds of business cards that had all the information on how to order my book to everyone I came across which sold a lot of books. During this time, I also learned that E.C.'s murder was the most famous unsolved murder of an OU student in the history of the University.

Joe and I were having so much fun that we started looking for some dates when we could do some book signings together outside of Norman when OU wasn't playing. I was going to ride his coattails as long as he let me and our first event was in Edmond, Oklahoma, at Best of Books. Nan Hight, the owner, had set it all up. I'd just finished reading Joe's book, *The Seven Secrets of the Silver Shoes* and after all the book signings we had done we were very comfortable together. We talked about our kids and Joe's first grandchild who had just been born, mostly family stuff. We both had some ideas about marketing our books and it was in one of those conversations I told him my idea for a film based on my book. Joe had a documentary of the highlights of his career which he showed at book signings whenever he could. Why not put one together about Chub and me? Since I'd always filmed Chub and myself during our conversations I had plenty of material to work with.

As the football season ended my interest in making a film grew and for the next several months I went to every film festival I could, educating myself about the business.
The Telluride Film Festival in Colorado was the first. Telluride is one of the leading festivals in the world for new film releases and it was easy to see why everyone loved coming there.
The town has an extraordinary setting, nestled in the mountains and surrounded by wildlife. The air is so pure it is almost intoxicating and despite the crowds who attend the festival the area is extremely peaceful. The entire town was packed, even the small campground where I was staying in a tent.

Telluride was an eye-opening experience for me, I got to see a lot of different films and I also rubbed elbows with many big-name actors and directors. The four-day festival went by in a hurry and by the time I got back to Oklahoma I was determined to make my own film.

Operating with only the money from book sales I found a guy in Bartlesville to help me with the editing who I could afford. He wasn't a film editing specialist but he convinced me he could do it and the next week I started the long editing process. I had thousands of feet of film, some of poor quality due to my inexperience in operating my camera or bad lighting. On weekends I traveled from one tradeshow to another always staying in second rate hotel, eating cheap food to save money and during the week I worked on the film. It seemed I was always spending more money than I brought in so I decided to buy a small motor home to cut costs.

All I needed was something I could sleep in. It would save all those weekend hotel bills maybe even some of my meal expenses. I'd been throwing the idea around in my head for a few weeks when I saw the perfect rig parked behind a house in Dewey. It was a 20-foot Volkswagen Rialta. I'd never heard of it before but the thing had a real bed, a shower, and a toilet and it fit in a regular parking space. It was exactly what I needed. After a little research I found Winnebago had made them for just a few years back in the late 1990s and they were a bit of a collectors' item. The one I was looking at still belonged to the original owner who was now in his late 80s and after I inquired he decided he might sell it to me. After a phone call to the bank I bought it on the spot and a couple of weekends later I was sleeping in it. The Rialta was working out great, even better when I had one of those fancy wraps put on the rig advertising the book.

Joe had invited me to the upcoming football season with him again in Norman and I figured this year I'd park the Rialta right on Campus Corner and with the advertising on it I expected another good year. Two months away from the first game, it occurred to me to take the Rialta to New York City. I'd been passing out cards all over the four-state area so why not do it where there were 17 million people and someone in the film business might get hold of the story. I was a rolling billboard in that Rialta. I had a place to sleep and plenty of time before OU's season started so I made a quick decision and the following week I was heading up the highway again although this time it would take three days of driving to reach my destination. Sticking to the major highways the drive went well as I spent most nights at truck stops where the sound of dozens of idling diesel engines put me to sleep.

My plan was to first drive up to the north shore of the Long Island Sound to a town called Guilford, Connecticut where I knew some people I thought could help me if I got into a bind. It was about a three-hour drive from Guilford into Manhattan and the heart of the entertainment district. All the major TV networks are there and it's also home to movie stars, professional sport franchises, Times Square, everything is right there in New York City. I planned to drive my little motor home continually through the heart of town handing out business cards. At night I'd drive down on the Northwest Highway that runs along the waterfront. I'd been in that area of the city before on other business and had seen plenty of overnight parking spaces where I thought I could stay. I could shower and sleep in the Rialta and cruise the streets during the day and just maybe get lucky. Stranger things had happened and I figured that between my driving time and that first OU football game I would have about two weeks in the city. By then if nothing happened I would start heading back toward Norman.

While in New York I needed to look up a couple of people and one in particular was Bob Wyatt. I'd gotten Bob's name from one of my readers who had thought he might be able to help me. In his younger years Bob had worked for several major publishers and had also been a successful writer. Now he was semi-retired, splitting his time between an apartment in New York City and a house in Woodstock, New York. Before I left Oklahoma, I phoned him explaining who I was and he gladly agreed to meet me at his apartment when I got to town. I was looking forward to seeing him and as I pulled off Highway 95 at the Guilford exit I had every little detail of my trip laid out. But first I needed to check in with my friends the Nortons who lived in Guilford to let them know I was here.

They were expecting me and I was pulling into their drive when I heard a sound like a short whistle coming from somewhere under the hood. Maybe it was my imagination or I had run over something but I was so happy to see these folks again I tried to forget it. Reminiscing about how we'd met led to dinner and an overnight stay in their guest bedroom which was a welcome change for me. Unfortunately, that whistle sound I'd heard stayed with me and I decided the next day instead of going on into New York I'd have a mechanic friend of the Nortons take a look at it. You can't get lucky all the time and for me this was one of those times. Not a belt or a tire it was my worst nightmare the transmission. When the mechanic pulled the pan, he found metal shavings which meant big trouble ahead for me. He could make some adjustments and adding some special fluid might keep me going awhile but a major overhaul was definitely in the future for the Rialta. It would also mean quite a bit of money. When the mechanic put the transmission back together and assured me it would run awhile longer I decided that after coming so far, I would continue with my trip. I got into Manhattan without any problems but as I put my driving plan into action the thought that it could all end quite quickly if the transmission started acting up was always on my mind.

I usually got started before daylight, driving up and down Times Square then making a loop by the CNN News headquarters building. At the early morning NBC Today show

I got noticed and talked briefly to Al Roker and Matt Lauer on the air live. Then later I visited with Matt who promised to take a closer look at the book I gave him. CBS was the same when after holding up a sign about the book one of the show producers promised to check it out. I drove around Central Park throughout the afternoons and then went around the banking district later in the day. This was my routine every day, two hours in the morning driving down Times Square past the TV news talk shows and if I got in a traffic jam somewhere I didn't care. The rolling billboard was doing the work if only I could keep it running.

I was a week into my schedule when my appointment with Bob Wyatt came around. By now I knew Manhattan a bit and I easily found his apartment where we visited for a couple of hours before deciding to go for a walk. Bob wanted to hear it all; how the Mullendores had accumulated all this land and how Gene Mullendore built the 300,000-acre Cross Bell empire, E.C.'s murder and Chub being on the run for 16 years and all the trouble he got into. As we walked time flew by. It was the middle of the summer and although I was drinking a lot of water I was covered in sweat and so was Bob. He was a good 20 years older than me and after we had walked several miles we decided to take the subway back to his apartment. It was three flights down to our train and once we entered the car I noticed Bob was in trouble. The only thing he said was that he felt dizzy and as I grabbed his arm he went limp but because the train was so full of people his body just stood there. This guy was having some kind of medical problem but when I called out for some assistance I got none. I didn't know what to do and Bob's stop was coming up. We had to get off there so as the doors opened I grabbed him around the chest and just pushed my way through the crowd yanking the emergency cord to keep the doors open. Once outside on the platform although there were many people around still no one offered to help.

The only thing I knew for sure was that this was Bob's stop and his apartment was a block away but first we would have to climb three flights of stairs straight up. I threw my arm around his waist and put his arm around my neck, dragging him up the stairs which brought a little life into him. Once above ground he told me he felt he could walk and with my assistance we headed toward his apartment. The doorman helped me get him to his room where I stayed with him for a couple of hours to make sure he would be okay. I needed the time to recover myself and as I poured water down my throat Bob thanked me profusely for my help. It had been quite a day for me and that night I would have a second encounter with trouble.

There were many homeless people staying in the area where I was spending my nights down on the Northwest Highway. Tents could pop up just about anywhere and at any time. Some nights I'd go to sleep with not a tent in sight and then the next morning I'd wake up and they'd be everywhere. Although most of these people were friendly I avoided contact with them. Some people asked for money and others could be hostile for no reason. The trick was to call their bluff. If money was asked for be polite but don't give it to them. Often, I would see the same people at night and it usually worked with them. I was feeling pretty comfortable after spending half a dozen nights in the same spot but on the same day Bob had his medical episode that changed.

It was late in the evening by the time I got back from Bob's to where I'd planned to stay that night. I was running the generator which was built into the Rialta watching the evening news on my little TV when someone started knocking on my door. This had happened before, with people wanting food or money and when I hollered out to go away they would usually leave but not this time. The knocking continued and as I refused to open the door I thought whoever it was out there was going to tear something up on the Rialta when they started pounding on the side of the vehicle. Whenever I'm traveling I always carry a .38 pistol which I'm licensed for in Oklahoma and most other states. I had it in my hand when I opened the door and although scared I showed no fear. Standing in front of me shaved-headed with tattoos all over his face and neck the man held a Bowie-style knife which at a quick glance appeared to be at least a foot long. With a foul mouth he demanded my money then attempted to peak in. As he did I quickly raised my gun and pulled the trigger back, sticking it to the side of his head. Watching his knife all the time, I said "Come get it you piece of shit!" It all happened in an instant as he backed away laughing saying he'd be back. I shouted that I'd be waiting but as soon as he was out of sight I was gone, down the Northwest Highway to another spot where that night I got little sleep.

My time in the city was running out and after some kids spray painted the Rialta one night and another night when I lost one of my mirrors and a hub cap I decided I'd had enough. I'd stuck it out for almost two weeks and as I headed home I felt the trip had been productive. While I was driving down the I-80 turnpike in Pennsylvania I felt the transmission slip a little after I stopped for gas. Once in high gear it seemed to run okay but when I stopped again a few hours later the slipping had gotten worse. It happened whenever I stopped for gas and it was becoming increasingly worse. From Ohio then Illinois until outside St. Louis where after a gas stop I just couldn't get it to take off. I had a full tank of gas which I thought was enough to make it home if I could just get the old Rialta rolling and pushing it by hand off to the side at the station I was sitting dead in the water when a guy in a wrecker pulled up asking if he could help. Explaining my problem, I offered him a $50.00 bill for a push. I didn't know if it would work but 15 minutes later he was behind me going almost 50 miles an hour. The transmission kicked into high and since I'd already paid him I just waved when he passed me. From St. Louis to

Springfield, then on to Joplin, knowing I might never get going again I couldn't stop even for rest area breaks. When I exited at Vinita even though I didn't have one I took the Pike Pass lane at high speed and got away with it. The Rialta had less than a quarter-tank of gas and I had a good hour-and-a-half to go. I was close enough to home now to call AAA for a tow but I didn't need it. Two days later minus the Rialta I was back in Norman telling Joe all about the trip.

Through Joe I had made many new contacts and most recently he had introduced me to Thomas Lott the great quarterback of the late 1970s at OU. Thomas had just released a book about his life and based on Joe's recommendation wanted to try a few tradeshows with me. His book was called *Getting into the Game: A Parent's Guide to Raising an Athlete*. A small paperback it got into the ups and downs of high school, college and pro sports. Thomas had played at every level and felt the need to tutor young athletes. It was a noble cause and when we were together I saw Thomas give away more books than he sold something Joe often did as well.

I admired their generosity but with my financial situation I wasn't able to do that.

I was working seven days a week either at book signings, restocking the stores that sold my book or going to all the football games I could. Internet sales were good especially when I was on the road promoting the book. When I returned from New York I went back to working on the documentary which I thought could help book sales and also gain some exposure for the project in the movie industry. Libraries around the state purchased multiple copies and there was one bookstore in particular that constantly sold out of books.

Brace Books in Ponca City, Oklahoma, was one of a dying breed of small independently owned bookstores. Jerry Brace had been selling books for 35 years in Ponca City when I delivered his first order. As is common with many bookstore owners, he planned to pay me when the books were sold. Two days later I got a call from Jerry asking for more books and saying he'd have a check waiting for me from the first bunch of books. Amazingly, this had been going on to the point where I expected a call from Jerry every week or so. Two hundred, four hundred, six hundred it was wild and Jerry was still selling more. After *The Oklahoman*, Oklahoma City's major newspaper, listed *Footprints in the Dew*, as the bestselling book in the state several weeks in a row Jerry wasn't the only one selling books.

The OU football season was half over and I had just finished putting the film together when I got an offer from Thomas Lott to join him and Coach Barry Switzer on game days. They do a live TV show called "Coach's Cabana," which is filmed either at Barry's house during away games or on Campus Corner during home games. It was an opportunity I couldn't refuse so Joe and I changed our book signing at Balfour to another day before each home game. This allowed me to be at Balfour with him and with Barry and Thomas on Saturdays for the game. Thomas and his wife Beth who worked at the State Capitol were very helpful to me. Now I found myself hanging out at Barry Switzer's house handing out cards and watching the game live on multiple big screen TVs while Barry and Thomas did their commentary. The show was called "Coach's Cabana" because it had started out in Barry's back yard under his cabana and it was in the ninth year. Revered by millions of fans, Switzer now 80 years old had done it all in football. After starring in high school and college, he coached OU to a couple of national championships then went on to the pros becoming the head coach of the Dallas Cowboys and winning a Super Bowl.

Barry had retired from coaching years before but under Coach Bob Stoops, OU's football team had continued to be very successful. Over the summer Stoops had also retired. Now the Sooners were being coached by Offensive Coordinator Nathan

Riley and expectations for the season were running high.

Because he was so well known, Joe always drew a crowd to Balfour never hesitating to give me a plug when we were there together. In Norman, just a block away from the stadium where he had played, Joe Washington was just a little below God in OU fans' eyes. Other past players and coaches would stop by to visit with him, which increased the size of the crowd helping books sales.

After we did our book signing Teddy Lehman would host his live radio show with more guests and commentary about the upcoming game. He knew about my book and on several occasions went out of his way to mention it, giving me more exposure every week. During my Saturday gig I finally got a chance to visit with Coach Switzer. I had watched this living legend from afar the first year Joe and I signed books together and I'd been introduced but so had hundreds of other people. Now I had become friendly with Thomas Lott, Barry's co-host on his TV show, which brought me to his attention.

Coach, as his past players call him, told me he knew the Mullendore clan and he had known Katsy's former husband John Mecom the owner of the New Orleans Saints well at the time of E.C.'s murder. He went on to tell me how much he liked the family and remembered how generous they had been. He added that he'd like to have a copy of my book and I couldn't run back to my car fast enough to get it for him.

I had a lot going on and on top of it the film was almost completed so I needed to find places for screenings.
The response was very positive from all the theaters in the area that I contacted. I decided that my first showing would be strictly a fundraiser for some needy local community and after looking at several options Sedan, Kansas, stuck out. It was the county where Chub's 1990 pot bust happened and his 16-year run from the law began and it was also where law enforcement brought him after his capture in Helena, Montana. Television

personality Bill Curtis owned property in the county and had always wanted to talk to Chub but the big draw for me was the people of the small town.

I'd become friendly with their senior citizens group when I did a couple of book signings in town with my friend Doris "Coke" Meyer who was 95 at the time and had written a memoir about her uncle Will Rogers. I'd noticed the old town theater before and after inquiring about it found that it was still open on weekends. This place was the real deal and still an operating theater. The community had come together to save it adding a new roof and more recently a new projection system. It had been a real beauty in its day and the original exterior and interior were still preserved. After contacting the senior group about my idea to show the film for the very first time in their theater and donate the proceeds, a date was set. The theater only held 150 people but at $10.00 a ticket plus concessions the senior organization thought it would be one of the biggest fundraisers they had ever had. I was excited for them as well and gave the event a lot of free publicity in my weekly column that unbelievably now had been running close to 17 years. With my other obligations in Norman with Joe and Thomas on game day weekends along with book signings and some more editing work on the film, the Sedan show snuck up on me.

Unfortunately, on the day of the screening it became obvious the film needed some cleaning up. There was lots of background noise and the sound skipped here and there but if you had ever doubted that Chub shot E.C. you could hear him confessing plain as day and that's what people came for. The theater was sold out when I got to Sedan and they told me it had been a sell-out for a couple of weeks, wanting to know if they could have a second showing that night. I was glad to do it and when I left Sedan that evening I felt great. I hadn't made anything on the film but I did sell some books and made a lot of friends.

The next week I was scheduled to show the film at the

Tulsa Historical Society where again I wasn't charging any fee but hoping to sell books. When I scheduled the showing with the Society's director she had anticipated a crowd of maybe 50 people. Arriving in Tulsa that morning from an Oklahoma City tradeshow I found that the 50 the director had expected had turned into close to 300 and there was a line outside the door. Three showings would be offered that day and they all sold out. As in Sedan the proceeds went straight to the Society's bank account.

The Poncan Theater another historic theater still in operation in Ponca City would be my next stop. With Brace Books unbelievably still selling lots of books I figured on a crowd and I wasn't disappointed. I liked donating the revenue from the ticket sales to these old theater houses but I was only making a couple of dollars from each book I sold at these events so when the theater manager from the Poncan offered to split the door I accepted.

The next showing was scheduled at the historic Coleman Theater which was built back when Route 66 was the main highway and ran right through Miami. In recent years the theater has been meticulously restored and today even the original organ is back in place. It snowed heavily all day and into the evening on the day of the screening and I wasn't sure what to expect. The theater manager had advertised the film throughout the area both on the radio and in newspapers and I had given several interviews about the project as well. Despite my misgivings about the weather several hundred people showed up, most of whom also bought books. Everywhere I went people liked the film and I always followed a screening with a question-and-answer time. A bit uneasy at first, by the time I hit Miami I was starting to feel more comfortable in front of a crowd.

I was still working with the original guy who had helped me put the film together but my patience had about run out with him because at every screening the film would have a glitch. Each time he tried to fix one problem another one would pop up. I had scheduled two important showings in Tulsa; a return engagement at the Historical Society and then a week-long showing at another historical theater, the Circle Cinema and I needed the film to be in perfect condition. After visiting with a couple of other folks who were involved in filmmaking I finally figured out that this fellow was just milking me for more money and possibly doing things to the film on purpose. The showing at the Tulsa Historical Society would turn out to be the last straw when again the glitches were not cleaned up. Fortunately, the film was in good enough shape to show and the following week it opened at the Circle Theater.

The film drew a large crowd at the Cinema and everyone enjoyed it but all I could concentrate on were those little mistakes that seemed to get bigger and bigger every time I saw them. The next day I made an appointment to see the film guy, telling him I wanted all my material erased from his system and then I would pay him anything I owed him. Up until now he had always been very pleasant but when I confronted him about the problems with his work he became openly hostile. I had finally seen through him; this 40-year-old punk just wanted a paycheck and despite claiming to be a devout Christian he didn't hesitate to cuss me out. I was disappointed in him but more so in myself. I had become engrossed in working on the film and had let my guard down.

Now I had another problem, the film still needed additional editing and I didn't have a technician to do it. I had been talking with Joe Washington about my dilemma and he had suggested someone but that person turned out to be busy. Others I interviewed just weren't right for the job. I spent a lot of money working with several different firms and the quality of the film improved but still wasn't perfect.

It had been close to a year since Katsy and I had spoken when I heard that her husband Jim had died and she was sick herself. Our last conversation had been about a local man who was obsessed with the Mullendore family, sending letters to Katsy and her family and lurking outside the main gate trying to get onto the ranch. Given everything she had been through she was very concerned that he was a menace to all of them and asked me to look into his background. I contacted the Osage County Sheriff's department and discovered that the man was from Bartlesville and had suffered a serious breakdown, ending up in a mental institution. After many years he had just been released. I decided to follow him for several weeks and after I did I determined that he was not an immediate threat to anyone. However, the Sheriff's department was not convinced and they conducted their own surveillance which gave Katsy some peace of mind.

Katsy and Jim had been very fair to me the entire time I'd been involved in solving E.C.'s murder and writing the book and I had been happy to help her with this problem. They had asked me for my discretion and I'd been able to fulfill their request. During our last conversation she had thanked me for all I'd done and wanted to make sure we were square. I had a premonition then that her time on earth was short and when she died I knew I'd never see someone with so much class ever again in my life. I wished many times I'd gone ahead and included more in the book about the Mullendores' generosity and the kind things E.C.'s friends had told me about him but I honored Katsy's wishes.

I am hoping that someday a real movie will be made out of this story about cowboys and cattle, a western about what it took to build a mighty ranch in the early days of statehood in Oklahoma. The filmmakers might throw in the murder of the heir to this dynasty and the life of the man who kept a secret for fifty years.

As the lights dim in the theater it's September 26, 1970, a cool, peaceful evening out on the Cross Bell ranch with only the sound of a few night birds singing. Then shots ring out from E.C. Mullendore III's house the beginning of a turbulent time for the Mullendore family. But by the time the lights come up in the theater Katsy has finally learned the truth about the death of her brother and so has the audience.

THE PHOTOS

BEFORE THE DEW

As far back as I can remember when I wasn't in school, Pittsburg, Kansas was my home. This is where we milked the cows by hand. My grandfather was a union welder and also did a lot of jobs on the side; to the left is his welding shop. A smoker and a bit of a whiskey drinker, he died from a heart attack in his middle fifties. After that my grandmother sold the farm and moved into town. She herself died three years later.

I was at loose ends following the sudden death of a close friend. There was nothing keeping me in Oklahoma so I bought this used truck and an old camper and headed for the East Coast. Starting in the Chapel Hill, North Carolina area, after a few months I moved north with no particular destination in mind. I lived there off and on for the next few years, usually working construction. When I reached Maine after two years I still had the same rig.

Madison, Connecticut, on the north shore of Long Island Sound, is a popular summer destination for tourists. While I was working on a construction project there, I got the idea to set up a roadside food business. I found a spot along Route One where there was plenty of traffic passing by and I built a large meat smoker from an old metal drum. With all the required permits in hand, in the summer of 1994 I opened "Smoklahoma". At the time, most Connecticut folks had never had smoked meat before and the business was immediately successful. I served a couple of different meats for lunch everyday along with side dishes and also took a lot of custom orders for ribs, whole chickens, ducks, turkeys and brisket. By the end of the summer season I was exhausted after working seven days a week usually twelve hours a day. I was never so happy as when my meat supplier offered to buy the business but people continued to call me for orders for months afterwards.

In this photo I am in costume cooking for a private party at the famous Shubert Theater in New Haven, Connecticut. The Shubert was originally a try out house for plays and musicals before they went to Broadway and in fact *Oklahoma!* was partially written there. By this time the theater had become a not for profit performing arts but it was still showing Broadway productions featuring stars like Tommy Tune, Robert Goulet and Marie Osmond. Through my writing coach I made a connection there and occasionally worked security for some of the performers.

The electronic billboard in front of the Bartlesville Community Center read Riders in the Sky, Saturday March 20th, 7PM. Dinner at 5PM. Dance at 9PM. At this point in my life I had a sideline booking bands. The Fabulous Midlife Crisis Band was my personal favorite but I also enjoyed bringing acts like *Riders in the Sky* and Vince Gill to Bartlesville.

In 2006 I had been writing a weekly column for the local newspaper in Bartlesville and a couple of other papers in Kansas for several years. When fugitive Damon "Chub" Anderson was arrested in Helena, Montana after sixteen years on the run from law enforcement in Oklahoma and Kansas, I was determined to cover the story.

Chub is seen here leaving the courtroom after pleading guilty to pot cultivation charges. The film crew from Bill Kurtis' show America's Most Wanted is standing close by as Chub is led to a waiting car that will eventually take him to Lansing Prison. This was our second meeting and it would not be the last as I went on to see him at the prison every week until his release.

In the section of the town cemetery reserved for Lansing Prison inmates lie two of the most well-known killers in American history whose story was made famous by Truman Capote. Richard Hickock and Perry Smith lived together, killed together, were hung minutes apart on the same day and are now buried together. In an eerie coincidence I learned from the assistant warden that Chub was being held in a cell formerly occupied by Hickock.

I traveled the country and went to every high-profile event I could in hopes of getting someone in the film industry interested in making a movie about a forty-year-old murder. Every year the National Cowboy & Western Heritage Museum in Oklahoma City hosts the Western Heritage Awards and I have met many fascinating people there. After visiting with actor, musician and poet Red Steagall about my project, he told me that Katsy Mullendore Whittenburg was a personal friend of his and that she had given him the best horse he had ever owned.

I was in New York City, performing rope tricks in front of the CNN office when I met Geraldo Rivera. He was kind enough to listen to my story and asked me to keep him up to date.

At the big Telluride, Colorado Film Festival I had the opportunity to run into many different people in the film and TV industry including film critic Leonard Matlin from Entertainment Tonight. The festival has been going on for 45 years and draws thousands of people to this scenic, small town. With no money for a high dollar hotel room, I found camping twelve miles outside of town with no water or electric just fine and I had plenty of company both human and animal.

Ernest Borgnine knew about the murder and wanted to play E.C.'s dad Gene in any film adaptation of my book. His interest wasn't an act and he would have been perfect but unfortunately, he died a few months after we spoke.

I made several trips to New York to promote the book and was lucky enough to set up meetings with several important people in the media. None was more important than Rikki Kleinman, a long time CBS News correspondent who was married to the NYC Police Commissioner at the time, Bill Bratton. Rikki and I had met during the Whitey Bulger trial in Boston and whenever I was in town she found time to have breakfast with me. I will always be grateful for her advice and moral support.

I've crossed paths with actor Tom Selleck several times. On this occasion he was the guest of honor at the Western Heritage Awards. Although he was mobbed by fans throughout the event, I still found him very approachable.

Three very accomplished people, each in their chosen field.

On the left football icon Joe Washington who not only has two national championship rings from his college career at the University of Oklahoma but who also went on to play pro ball and helped the Washington Redskins win the Super Bowl.

In the center is Janine Regier a world class Women's Cart Class driver who has won shows across the country, exceling in competitions where horse and driver must truly act as a team.

On the right is rancher, business executive, professional sports franchisee owner and philanthropist Bob Funk. There is not enough space here to list all of Bob's many achievements and I'm quite sure I'll never meet another person like him.

Many people have supported me during the research and writing of *Footprints in the Dew* but my biggest champion has always been Bob Funk. I have disliked flying for years but on this day, I decided if this was the way I was going to meet my maker what better company to have than Bob.

In the second row from the bottom, the fourth boy from the right is pledge E.C. Mullendore III. Usually the first to pitch in on cleaning day, E.C. was well liked by everyone I've talked to who knew him during his days at the University of Oklahoma. He often took his fraternity brothers home to the Cross Bell Ranch to hunt and fish.

BEFORE THE DEW

THE COLUMNS

These chapters are for everyone who has read *Footprints in the Dew* and still has questions about who killed E.C. Mullendore III. For those of you with any doubts, I believe the weekly columns I wrote about the murder and the letters from Chub and Katsy will give you some more insight into the story.

My column ran for over 15 years and I covered many topics. I have edited the columns that appear here, taking out the material that isn't relevant to this story.

The two columns at the end of this section are about the various places where I first wrote the manuscript for *Footprints in the Dew* and later *Before the Dew*. I found these places to be very inspirational and I also received a lot of support from the staff at each one.

Looking for the Truth

Welcome back. For the past five years I have been on a journey that started quite simply.

On Wednesday July 5, 2006 I was at the Chautauqua County, Kansas courthouse hoping to get an interview with Damon Tucker "Chub" Anderson. Anderson had been on the run for 17 years after skipping bond for a drug bust and he had been on the Kansas Most Wanted List the entire time. He had finally been captured in Montana on June 2nd and was transferred back to Kansas to face the original charges.

Bill Kurtis from America's Most Wanted was also in the courtroom with his film crew as were retired Osage County Sheriff George Wyman and Osage County Sheriff Department Investigator Dwight Barnard. There was also a handful of newspaper reporters and a crowd of roughly 75 onlookers some of whom were Chub's friends and some who merely wanted to get a look at the famous fugitive. I was in the courtroom when he pled guilty to those charges and what followed was the meeting that began our relationship.

Anderson had been angered by remarks Kurtis had made to him in a closed-door meeting and after I was introduced to him in a hallway outside the courtroom he asked if I would like to meet with him again. Of course, I wanted to but where would be the question. Earlier in the day he had been sentenced to 1-5 years in prison and it would be a challenge to find out which prison he would sent to. In addition, I would have to be approved by the warden of that prison in order to go inside the walls.

As it turned out Anderson's new "home" was the historic Lansing State Penitentiary and before long he began sending me letters about his life there. Our correspondence lasted about a month until I cleared all the background checks required to visit him. For the rest of his stay at Lansing I saw Chub every weekend conducting a long series of one on one interviews.

Truman Capote had done the same thing in his quest to get the true story from Richard Hickcock and Perry Smith which he recounted in *In Cold Blood* and I have followed somewhat in his footsteps.

Till next time I'll see ya down the road

Behind the Walls – Part I

Welcome back. This week will be the start of an adventure that will take you behind the walls of the oldest penitentiary in the Kansas/Oklahoma territory – dating back to the days when Oklahoma sent their inmates to Kansas to be imprisoned.

You'll be with notorious inmates Richard Hickock and Perry Smith and hear how Truman Capote moved around freely behind the prison walls. You'll also learn how life is for Chub Anderson and his strange crossing of fate with Hickock and Smith. You'll visit the old prison cemetery which Walter Cronkite comes to every year and learn why and meet a Supreme Court Justice along the way. We'll go on location to what was the largest cultivated marijuana crop field in the state, find out how it was discovered and interview several of the people involved including the growers. You'll meet Rudy Briggs who was one of the first sheriff's investigators on the scene of the Mullendore murder in this made-for-the-big-screen real life mystery.

So, fill up your canteen and come along with me to Lansing Kansas for the first installment of the *Original Buffalo Dale Behind the Walls*.

It's July 27, 2006 and we're being searched by the first of many guards we'll face on entry. No phones or smoking materials are allowed and naturally no guns, knives or weapons of any type. And no cash can be taken into the prison. Money is not needed inside these confines and you will be searched coming out also. The thought is that visitors might be laundering money for the inmates.

After being processed I am issued a badge to be worn at all times, my hand is stamped with invisible ink and my license is returned to me to be kept handy throughout my visit. I am told to take a seat in the waiting area where I meet two men who are being released that morning and are waiting for a bus that will take them to anyplace they choose in Kansas. I don't have to wait long but I have time to visit with one of the two inmates who told me about the bus ticket, the $100 "gate money" every inmate receives when released and the games you have to play to survive behind the walls. The anxiety of this young man is clearly visible and he says that waiting for the bus to arrive is the worst. He just wants to taste his freedom. I wish him well as Brett Petersen, Executive Officer to the warden arrives and my journey inside Lansing Correctional Facility begins.

Our first steel door opened and my driver's license was required to proceed. Then we walked down a long hallway to a set of steel bars where my hand was swiped under an infra-red blue light. Next, I moved through another set of steel gates where my ID badge was scanned. Now I'm standing in an island like place where they have their own system of rules that you live by. The thought of someone coming up behind you is ever constant as you look at the inmates who are moving around freely, going about their business. It takes some getting used to but as we head to the industrial area Brett's manner is so professional that my fears drift off and before long my blood pressure goes back down and I am peppering Brett with questions again.

Our first stop is the toy shop where some of the finest woodworking I've ever seen is done, creating toys for not-for-profit and government fund raising events and for distribution to underprivileged children. Next door is a laser design shop where men are doing some extraordinary work making signs and other products. Then comes the paint and metal working shop where all the Kansas State highway signs are made and the paint is produced for the highways and school buses. There is also an embroidery shop which makes all the hats for the NCAA, the NFL, major league baseball teams and companies such as Gear and Sprint. In addition, there are several other smaller shops that make goods of various kinds, all with inmate labor. It is quite fascinating and keeping these men busy I believe is the reason this area seems so tranquil. There are several private companies that work inside the walls and supply "civilian" crew bosses who teach the inmates how to operate the machinery and provide them with a trade if they don't have one.

At any given time, there are 500-600 men working in the industrial division on three 8-hour shifts – 24 hours a day if needed. They are paid minimum prevailing wage to start and 25% goes back to the penitentiary for room and board. 10% is put into mandatory savings, a small amount is paid into each inmate's commissary account and the balance is paid into a victims' restitution fund.

Next, we go into the C unit where disruptive inmates are housed in segregated cells to maintain the security of the prison. You don't want to go here and my impression is that you'd better be tough if you're working in this area. My hat goes off to the guards securing these men. On average a guard works about three years before deciding either to leave or make this their career. If they stay they begin to work their way up the chain of command as warden Dave McKune and Brett Petersen have done – two fine dedicated men. While I'm talking about the guards- there are 463 working three shifts here watching over the 2,400 inmates in residence. This works out to about 154 guards on each shift. My blood pressure is going up again! I'd better take a break. Next week "D" block, "H" block and the Safe Harbor prison Adopt-A-Dog program that Brett is involved with. It's a great story. Also coming up.– coal mining inmates, the clinic, maximum security "B" block and the Chub Anderson-Truman Capote connection. Until then official guest #938 will be seeing ya down the road….

Down the Road with the Original Buffalo Dale

Welcome back to Part II of "Buffalo Dale Behind the Walls." Before we get to "D" block I want to remind you that my paperwork hasn't been processed yet and there's a few more hoops to jump through before I get my second interview with Mr. Anderson. Also, at this point in time I had not read *In Cold Blood* or seen the new movie about Truman Capote and these things will have some meaning as we continue our tour.

"D" block is where the mules used to be housed back in 1879 when the inmates started mining for coal on the 2,538-acre prison property. Today there are around thirty miles of mine tunnels under the city of Lansing from this period. This section of the prison was later converted to inmate housing with wire mesh doors and block walls but you can still imagine the mules and coal mining prisoners who once occupied this area.

"H" block is our next stop where there is dormitory style housing and this is where Brett tells me about the Safe Harbor prison dogs. The inmates here all have a dog assigned to them from the local pound and they train them to sit, come, and stay. They housebreak, or in this case prison break the dogs and then adopt them out. At the present time 1,250 I must say very well-trained dogs have been adopted. I was very impressed with all the inmates here and if you're interested in adopting a dog from their program here is their website: www.safeharbor-prisondogs.com You'll get a great dog and what a story to tell your friends. You can also call my new friend Laura Philippi for more info at (913) 250-0203.

My blood pressure takes an upward spike here as Brett's radio started getting some chatter going and before you know it all the cell doors close, guards are scrambling and I am locked in. There's been a security breach and I'm thinking about an inmate takeover but wait – I've been watching too many movies. It's a false alarm and before you know it things are back to normal. Brett doesn't blink an eye and we move on.

As we walk toward the clinic, Brett is telling me more about the notorious Hickock and Smith story and about Truman Capote. The clinic provides dental & optical care, physical therapy, x-ray and laboratory work along with mental health crisis intervention counseling and psychological evaluations of the inmates. This is very good care for men that are in a bad situation in life.

Nearby is the maximum security "B" block. I want to mention that neither Brett nor the warden know who Chub Anderson is, to them he is just another man doing his time.

With that in mind this is where a strange thing happened.

I was following Brett into "B' block and listening to his Hickock and Smith stories when we stopped about 20 cells down the corridor. This is where Hickock and Smith must have been held before they were hung in 1965. Over the P.A. I hear "mess call, mess call". It is 12:30 PM and time for the prisoners in this section to be released for lunch. As I listen to the click, click, click, click of automatic locks opening, men start leaving their cells. They are putting on their clothes as they come out because it's over 100 degrees in the prison – no a.c. here and its hot! As Brett continues to talk, the door to one of these cells opens and a thin older man with a shaved head steps right out in front of me. I have to take a second and a third look to believe my eyes but yes, it is Chub Anderson pulling on his clothes less than 10 feet from me! I don't think he recognizes me and I interrupt Brett's story to mention that this is the man I'm trying to see. Brett is also quite amazed and he reminds me that I haven't been cleared for any conversation so I just watch Chub walk down to the cafeteria for lunch. His condition looks about the same as a couple of weeks ago as he walks away without speaking to anyone. Now the odds against my stopping at his cell at that time had to be astronomical – that out of 2,400 men I would run into Chub this way. It must have been fate.

But in any event, I obeyed the rules and Warden McKune appreciated it.

I am about out of space so the information that Warden McKune copied me on about Hickock and Smith and how Truman Capote was granted access to these two killers will have to wait until next week. But before I go here are a few quick facts about the Kansas State Penitentiary:

The prison was founded in 1859 and it is the largest and oldest prison in the state.

Until 1909 the prison also housed inmates from Oklahoma.

The prison has provided $1,098,680 in free community labor for many different state projects.

The ethnic breakdown of the prison population is as follows:

Caucasian............................59%
African American...............38%
Native American................2.2%
Asian....................................5%

The age breakdown of the prison population is:

19 and under.........................2%
20-29...................................29%
30-39...................................34%
40-49...................................25%
50-59.....................................8%
over 60...................................3%

The average age for a prisoner is 36 years old. The oldest inmate is 86 and the youngest is 16. Mr. Anderson will soon be 65.

Next week: they lived together, killed together, were hung together and they're buried together. Dick Hickock and Perry Smith- my behind the walls' scoop. Also coming up 20 tons of pot northeast of Dewey and my connection to landowner Pat Scudder.

Until then, released on good behavior at 2:10 PM July 27, 2006 one Original Buffalo Dale and I'll see ya down the road.

Behind the Walls – Part III

Welcome back to Part Three of "Buffalo Dale Behind the Walls."

Before I get to the scoop I want to lay out the time frame I will be referring to for those of you who haven't read *In Cold Blood* or seen the movie. On November 15, 1959 Mr. and Mrs. Herbert Clutter, along with their son Kenyon and their daughter Nancy were found bound, gagged and shot in the head in Gardner City, KS. Robbery appeared to be the motive although only a little over $40 was missing. A massive manhunt began but with few clues it quickly proved fruitless. Then on Friday, December 30,1959 31-year-old Perry Smith and 28-year-old Richard Hickock were arrested in Las Vegas for passing bad checks. After their arrest they were implicated in the robbery and murder of the Clutter family by a cellmate of Hickock's. The gun and knife used in the murders was found at Hickock's parents' home and the pair was sent back to Kansas. Truman Capote was already a well-known author when he learned about this story and it captured his imagination. It had all the elements of a great whodunit: innocent victims, hardworking lawmen, colorful townspeople and two bad guys. Capote turned this story into the most famous non-fiction book of the 1960s and some would say permanently changed the style of non-fiction reporting. A stick to the facts movie starring Robert Blake quickly followed and in 2005 the Oscar winning *Capote* was released which focuses on Truman Capote's experiences while writing the book. I could go on and on but space is limited so here are a few things that aren't in any movie that Warden McKune passed along to me from the Kansas City Star. According to *The Star* quote "Capote and Perry Smith became lovers in the penitentiary. I can't prove it but they spent a lot of time up there in the cell and Capote spent a considerable amount of money bribing the guard to go around the corner.

They were both homosexual and that is what happened." KBI Agent Harold Nye as told to George Plimpton in his 1997 book *Truman Capote.*

Capote himself said that as the rope was slipped over his head Smith's last words were directed to him: "Good-bye, I love you and I always have". You won't see this in the movies but that's the scoop.

I may have more reports from Lansing, KS. As I pursue my visits with Chub Anderson I find it is a fascinating little corner of the world. But let's get back to some closer soil north of Dewey where I had the chance to visit the site of Chub's 1980s garden.

On Friday I toured the area where the largest cultivated marijuana field in Oklahoma (at the time) was discovered. The crop was estimated at 2 tons and it was growing in a field as big as a football field that is watered by a tributary of Coon Creek. In the mid-1970s I worked on this ranch myself along with a good friend, horse trainer Steve Milligan. As young boys we fed cattle and horses, fixed fence and did all the other things that need done very day on a large ranch. Chub was living there at the time and I was always told to keep my distance from his house, which I did.

Chub was a good welder and the pipe corrals and out buildings he built are still standing along with the electric pole that powered the mobile room where he lived with his family: his second wife and his son from his first marriage. Chub and his second wife were married from 1972 to 1981. I've visited with her on two occasions and found her quite charming. She was a local girl who fell in love with the handsome and charismatic cowboy and wanted to make a family. When I mentioned that my adventures were taking me out to her old home her first thought was her old fruit trees and the garden she had kept. She was wondering if any of it still survived. As the granddaughter of US Marshall Charles Johnson from Indian

Territory days I could tell she is embarrassed by her involvement with this notorious case. She had never been in any trouble before this and has led a model life afterwards.

I've heard the field was discovered by a young man fishing along the creek who filled his pockets with his "catch" only to get busted a few days later. He told law enforcement officials the location of the field. This boy may have been a friend of Chub's son but whatever the case on August 6, 1980 Chub was arrested and his troubles with the law continued with another bust in Sedan in the 1980s at which time he decided to run.

Today the land has been returned to Bermuda grass but there's pot growing wild everywhere. It's easy to imagine that day in 1980 with news crews and photographers buzzing around – I wonder how many went home with full pockets themselves.

Till then I'll see ya down the road…

Chub and Gary Glanz

I think all of you who have been following this case will be interested in this article, particularly if you didn't see the piece in Oklahoma Magazine. Things may finally about to break in the next few months. Stay tuned.

Welcome back. The October issue of *Oklahoma Magazine* featured an article about unsolved murders in Oklahoma and in it private investigator Gary Glanz is quoted regarding the tragic beating and shooting death of E.C. Mullendore on September 26, 1970:

"We have got the answer. There was another man with Chub on the night of the murder who helped cover it up. I am working with the D.A. in Osage County to resolve it."

The article stated that an indictment could be pending.

Did Glanz get a death bed confession from Chub Anderson as he states in the article?

Did he and Anderson have the type of relationship that would lead Anderson to reveal his 40-year-old secret to Glanz? And if he did, why didn't the cops make an arrest if there was a co-conspirator in the murder as he stated. Well, this information and more may all come out in a new documentary that is scheduled to begin filming in the area next week. The film crew is from Australia and they produce a show with over 77 million viewers around the world which will be shining a light on this famous unsolved crime.

After I was subpoenaed by the Attorney General to appear before a multi county Grand Jury my own attorneys have recommended that I not comment on what I know or reveal my role in the story. What I can do is give you a little history on just who Gary Glanz is and how he came to be involved in this case.

Glanz started his career on the Tulsa Police force in the 1960s where he built a reputation for having a sixth sense about crime. Before long he decided that his true calling was in the

P.I. business and with not much more than his instincts he went into business for himself in the late '60s. He received a call from E.C. Mullendore's widow's attorney just four hours after the murder and the three of them drove out to the ranch together early the following morning. This was the start of Glanz's investigation of the murder, a crime he has said many times in print should have been solved within the first 72 hours.

"This was never a contract hit" he has stated, adding that he knew who killed E.C. and for $100,000 could prove that Mullendore had not committed suicide or arranged to have himself killed in order for his heirs to collect his life insurance. At the time his death benefit was thought to be the largest ever paid in the history of the insurance business. Although the murder investigation continued for the next three years, Glanz went on solving other cases and in 1973 the Wall Street Journal published a front-page profile of him calling him a "Super Sleuth" and the best P.I. in the southwest.

As you might expect from a man who thrives on getting the job done no matter what the cost, *Dirty Harry* is his favorite movie and the weapon he carries is a Browning 9MM 15 shot automatic customized with an inch and a half cut off the barrel and Smith& Wesson sights. He has said that he also packs a Walther 9MM 7 shot automatic and that neither gun has a safety. "If you're going to pull a gun you have two choices, use it or eat it." Now 72 years old, Glanz has traveled around the world working on everything from high profile cases to simple thefts and divorces usually solving his cases and solving the Mullendore murder would put the lid on his most famous case!

Till next week I'll see ya down the road....

Down the Road with the Original Buffalo Dale

Welcome back. Many people have asked me to comment on the recent newspaper article concerning Chub Anderson and the Mullendore murder. The following is my recollection of the time I spent with Chub, which I hope reflects my respect for all the parties involved in this tragedy.

It was July 5, 2006 when I had my first real visit with a man who had become a legendary figure in this part of the world. The wrinkles in his face showed he'd spent many a day outdoors in severe weather and his bowed legs spoke of hours on horseback. Several of his fingers were gnarled from various mishaps but he was still able to write. Captured with little but the clothes on his back and facing severe medical problems, much of his life was focused on sheer survival.

He first asked to meet with me after a chance encounter at his sentencing hearing in Sedan, Kansas and to this day I'm not sure why. There were plenty of reporters on hand who were willing to pay to gain his attention and his trust. His life experiences had taught him to read people through eye contact, facial expressions and body language. He could see right through people and understand their motives almost immediately. On many occasions I saw him quickly assess the people who came knocking on his door, some of whom were friends and some of whom were complete strangers. Regardless, they all called him Chub. That's how it was when we first met and that's how it was when he died.

After several months spent getting to know one another while he was incarcerated, I eventually agreed to make a trip to Alder, Montana. This is the small mountain town where he had been living for most of the last sixteen years before his capture.

In the time just before his arrest Chub had been living in one seedy hotel after another in Helena, Montana keeping his few remaining possessions in an old travel trailer which was stored on a friend's property high in the mountains outside of Alder, There were several boxes of handwritten notes and paperwork, old clothes and some home movies he had made of himself in better days. He'd bought the camera right after he went the run in 1990, fleeing the charges related to his most recent arrest for pot growing in Kansas. As a result, he had also violated his probation for similar charges in Oklahoma. He created a new life for himself as "Jack Everett" and managed to avoid capture for sixteen years. This is when he purchased a top of the line (for the day) movie camera and tripod to film what he would later describe "as the best time in my life."

Chub asked me to retrieve these films along with the boxes of paperwork and a few personals items. He kept a few clothes and left the rest with me to refer to while I was writing the story of his life.

Over time Chub told me about the most important things in his life; the good and the bad things he had done, his relationships with friends and lovers, his family and his enemies. In the months before his capture he hadn't had much company and later when he was paroled in Kansas and eventually moved into a small apartment, things didn't change much. I visited him several times a week to work on my project and I found there were a few people who were devoted to helping him but many others came to see him out of curiosity rather than genuine friendship. Chub could be charming to these people and would usually entertain them with well-practiced stories from the past.

Till next week I'll see ya down the road.....................

Ennis, Montana – Part I

Welcome back. Ennis is situated in Madison Valley, the southwestern corner of Montana, which is surrounded by three ranges of the Rocky Mountains: the Madison Range, Gravelly Range and the Tobacco Root mountains. People are drawn to the area from all over the world for the beautiful scenery and the outstanding hunting and trout fishing. Ennis is the biggest community in this part of Montana and on the opening day of hunting season the town puts on an all-day feed for the four to five thousand hunters who flock to the town to hunt for elk, mountain goat and deer. Trout fishing and hunting are the two mainstays of the local economy and the townspeople give their guests the red-carpet treatment. This new resident with his love of the outdoors would fit right in but he'd have to be careful.

The town has had its fair share of outlaws seeking a hideout including drug dealers and money launderers as well as the father and son who kidnapped Olympic athlete Kari Swenson and murdered one of her rescuers. In 1985 the local sheriff Johnny France became a legend when he tracked the two down alone and captured them in the mountains. He later wrote a book about his adventure that became a movie. Johnny France was still living in Ennis when Chub moved there. His adventures had made him a local celebrity but he had no way of knowing that one of Kansas' ten most wanted fugitives would soon be the next bad man taking refuge in the woods of Ennis.

Till next time I'll see ya down the road…

Ennis, Montana – Part II

Welcome back. This week's excerpt continues the profile of Chub's life on the run living under the assumed name of Jack Evert in Montana. I have drawn from both audio taped and video taped conversations I had with him as well as interviews with people he knew there.

Chub's first weeks were spent in an older motel on the edge of town- he needed a job and soon he heard about some work in the high-country town of Alder which was about forty miles west and straight up. In the spring the area cattlemen band together and lease large portions of government owned land for grazing. They form associations with names like Three Forks, Warm Spring and Black Butt. Together they drive herds of cattle into the mountain valleys and leave them for the summer – usually with just one hired hand watching over them.
That man covers a vast area on horseback trying to keep track of hundreds of cattle; doctoring, guarding the calves and generally trying to keep the herd safe from the many hazards of this wide-open country.

For Chub the solitude and privacy of the mountains was exactly what he was looking for during his first few summers in Alder and the hard work suited him just fine. There are many dangers for cattle in these mountains including porcupines which are numerous and are especially dangerous for young calves that sniff the slow-moving rodents out of curiosity and end up with a nose full of potentially deadly quills. The babies then try to nurse their mothers and end up sticking the quills into their milk bags. The mothers won't let the babies eat and the next thing you know the cowboy has two sick animals, one of whom weighs at least 1,000 pounds and has to be roped and tied down without the benefit of any pens. Ranchers were always looking for a widower or hermit-type person for this work and when they found a person with “Jack Evert’s” skills not many questions were asked.

Till next time I’ll see ya down the road………………

Paul Kelly

Welcome back. Over the past ten years I have included many biographies in this column, some of famous people that many of you may have heard of and just as many about people I have known personally and think have special stories. This is about a person who falls into the second category and who recently passed away.

I first met Paul Kelly in the summer of 2006. At just over 6 feet tall and about 180 pounds he was in excellent shape. Easy going and frequently smiling, Paul had a disposition that reminded me of Andy Taylor from Mayberry in the old Andy Griffith TV show and from the beginning I found him extremely likeable. Paul had grown up in the small Osage County town of Grainola, Oklahoma which is northeast of Ponca City on the Kansas border. When he was a kid his mother worked as a cook on Boots Adams' Foraker ranch which later became the Oklahoma Land and Cattle Company.

In 1969 Paul was 26 years old and had earned a degree in Animal Science from Oklahoma State University. In addition, growing up on a farm had given him plenty of practical experience in farming and livestock management. He had worked for several years at the Coddington Livestock Research Station before taking a position as a County Agent in Emporia and Chace counties in Kansas. This is where he was working when E.C. Mullendore III contacted him about running the farming operation on his massive Cross Bell Ranch. According to Paul "It was a good job and the Mullendores were good people to work for but it only lasted a year and a half."

I knew from prior research that Paul had managed thousands of acres of farm land on the Cross Bell and had been responsible for all the men and machines required to make it productive. Over the course of several taped interviews Paul confirmed the details of his work on the ranch and what he thought was his small role in the dramatic events that took place there in 1970.

As an employee of the ranch he had been questioned in the initial investigation but heard nothing from law enforcement until 2010 when Osage County investigators asked him to come into the Sheriff's office. Paul told me that during this meeting he was questioned for over an hour regarding the murder of E.C. Mullendore. At the time the investigators told him that the case was solved and arrest warrants had been written which were awaiting a judge's signature.

Paul had a good memory and gave me a thorough account of this meeting with investigators which was confirmed during my subsequent visit the next day to the sheriff's office.

It was after that when I told Paul that I had been subpoenaed by the Attorney General to appear before a multi county Grand Jury looking into the murder. I had also received an unauthorized visit from one of the grand jury members who told me that they had never received any of the documents or tape recording that I had been ordered to release to them. This gentleman wanted to review my information hoping that the case could be finally closed and justice done. This contact between a jury member and a witness was way out of bounds but soon after Paul and I discussed it, he discovered he had cancer. Although we stayed in touch his health became far more important than an unsolved murder from decades before.

All of this makes interesting reading but this small piece of history about a good man's departure from life certainly does not tell the whole story of Paul Kelly, a man who I wish I'd more time with.

Till next time I'll see ya down the road.........

The Cross Bell Incident – Part I

Welcome back. I am frequently asked if Footprints in the Dew might be made into a movie and of course I am hoping this will happen. In the meantime, this week and next I'll be bringing you the story of an early attempt to make a film about this famous murder which I learned about several years ago.

In 2006 I began interviewing a man named Dale Kurht who had been the ranch manager on the Cross Bell Ranch at the time of the murder. He had been the first person on the scene after a shot and bleeding Chub Anderson came running to his house.

Dale now lived in Arkansas, about a three-hour drive from my house, and he and I had been meeting a couple times a week for about a month. I had all of his work history and it was very impressive. Dale was a real cow man and had worked on several big outfits in his life. Now retired, he kept busy breeding and training border collies.

Much of our conversation over my previous three visits had focused on the details of the night of the murder. Things were going well and I anticipated that my fourth visit would be the same but it wasn't. When I arrived at Dale's house a large 2'x 2' cardboard box was sitting on his kitchen table. The box was full of papers, some in file folders, some in spiral note books and others just loose. There were photos and receipt along with what Dale said were his personal notes. When I asked about what he was giving me and why he had saved these things for so many years he just replied "I knew someone would come along".
It was obvious that it would take some time to review all of these materials which included all Dale's records of his work at the Cross Bell.

I took the box with me when I left that day and I soon discovered something in the papers I hadn't expected, the manuscript of a film that had been planned about the murder. In a separate binder there was a contract between Dale and a company called Filmworks. Dated December 8, 1981, the contract specified that Dale would work on the project as a consultant and would advise on details such as locations. The contract was signed by a famous actor and producer named Don Hawks.

According to Hawks official bio, he had appeared in lots of big films including the Grapes of Wrath, Sands of Iwo Jima, Stagecoach, Red River and El Dorado. Among his co-stars were John Wayne, Charles Bronson and Clint Eastwood. Hawks had also been in numerous television shows such as Gunsmoke and Bonanza and had appeared in commercials for Miller Beer and Marlboro cigarettes. Don Hawks was a big shot and a closer inspection of the contract revealed that the entire budget for the production was laid out down to the penny. There was also information about the investment company backing the film and a list of the actors who would potentially play the leading roles. The complete script was also in Dale's box and these are some of the details I discovered.

The film was going to be called "The Cross Bell Incident" and the script was written by Dianne S. Conyers. Several big-name actors had been chosen to play the principal characters in the drama. The role of patriarch Gene Mullendore was the first one mentioned and Rory Calhoun had been cast. Calhoun had appeared in movies with the biggest names in Hollywood of the time including Marilyn Monroe, Robert Mitchum, Lauren Bacall, Betty Grable and Susan Hayward.

Calhoun was a very big star and at 6'4" he was known to be a tough guy off the set as well. A high school dropout at 13, Calhoun got caught stealing a gun and then was arrested for robbing several jewelry stores and stealing a car as a boy. He did time in a federal prison and was also jailed in San Quentin in California. After his release, an accidental meeting with a director got him into the movie business.

Gene Mullendore was also known to be a tough man and to Don Hawks Calhoun must have seemed the perfect choice to play a man who had built a ranching empire with sheer determination.

Who did Don Hawks have in mind for Chub, E.C. and the other roles? Here's a hint, for Linda it's an actress who co-starred with John Wayne in Chisum and whose real-life husband was the star of the TV series Rat Patrol. I'll give you her name and all the others next week.

Till then I'll see ya down the road...........

The Cross Bell Incident – Part II

Welcome back. This week I'm bringing you the second part of the Cross Bell Incident.

It was December 8, 1981when Dale Kurht received his contract and the project synopsis from Filmworks. The script was included in his packet along with a list of the actors under consideration for each of the major roles.

In addition to Rory Calhoun who was to play patriarch Gene Mullendore, there were several actresses in the running to play E.C.'s wife Linda. According to a handwritten note in Dale's file Anne Archer was considered to be perfect for the part but she was already starring in "Waltz Across Texas". Barbara Horan was also mentioned but the biggest name was Lynda Day George. The5'8" beauty had been in the hit TV series "Mission Impossible" and also appeared on "Love Boat" and "Charlie's Angels". She had starred opposite John Wayne in "Chisolm" and had met her actor husband Christopher George on the set of "The Gentle Rain". At the time he was starring in the hugely popular World War II based series "Rat Patrol".

For the role of Gene's wife Kathleen Filmworks had focused on veteran film actress Lois Hall. Hall was part of director John Ford's legendary "Western Stock Company", a group who appeared repeatedly in his films. According to Wikipedia, over time this group included Will Rogers, John Wayne, Henry Fonda, Maureen O'Hara, James Stewart, Ben Johnson and John Carradine. Quite a group

Next week in Part 3, producer Don Hawk's pick to play E.C. will be coming up and his choice for Chub Anderson will surprise you.

Till next time, I'll see ya down the road..................

Dale Kurht

Welcome back. This week after all the comments I received about my story regarding the passing of Paul Kelly, I thought I'd start off with a profile of the man who was Paul's boss and the overall manager of both the farming operation and cattle production on the Cross Bell Ranch back in 1970.

I tracked Dale Kurht down in 2007 when he was living in retirement and training stock dogs in Arkansas. After I had visited with him several times, out of the blue he produced a large cardboard box filled with files and photographs documenting the time he had spent on the Mullendores' ranch.

As we looked through all of these materials, Dale told me that he had been hired in 1969 by E.C. Mullendore to help run the ranch. From the way he described it he had plenty of experience for the job. He came from four generations of farmers and ranchers and his great-grandfather had homesteaded the land Dale was born on. Dale was also a member of the American Hereford Association and a long time 4-H judge. He was managing the Codding Cattle Research Station near Foraker, Oklahoma when E.C. contacted him about the position. He said that when he was hired he thought nothing could touch the Cross Bell Ranch where he had heard the Mullendores themselves were not even sure how much land they controlled. Dale had been moving up the ladder, managing one large ranch after another, each one bigger than the one before. He had also worked at several big spreads outside of Oklahoma including the Milky Way Hereford Ranch in Phoenix, the Lucky Ranch in Loyalton, California and the Baca Grant Ranch in Moffat, Colorado.

In his line of work Dale told me this was the ultimate-the top of the heap – and he jumped at the chance to go to work for the Mullendores.

Dale's records indicated that there were thousands of head of cattle, hundreds of pigs and over fourteen hundred horses, a herd of Texas longhorns and several dozen free roaming bison on the Cross Bell. Another twenty-three race horses were stabled in Louisiana. It took sixteen feed trucks, eighteen full time men and a string of day laborers to work on all the different parts of the ranch. There were ongoing improvements being made to all areas of the operation including the construction of two Honegger houses for birthing pigs. Each house could hold 480 pigs, tripling the size of the hog operation. New shipping pens were being built along with fifteen miles of new fencing each year, a new fed lot, six new barns and an irrigation system that took care of four hundred and fifty acres where alfalfa would be planted. With over a thousand miles of fencing and cross fencing to be maintained and constant repairs to ranch vehicles, dozens of tractors and other ranch equipment I was surprised to find out how big the operation really was even though I had heard about the Cross Bell Ranch my whole life.

Paul Kelly and Dale had stayed in contact in the years following the tragic murder of E.C. Mullendore in 1970. Although they lived in different states I would often drive to both places in the same day to visit with both men and confirm details about their time on the Cross Bell while they were fresh in my mind.

I mentioned in last week's column that Paul had recently been questioned about E.C.'s murder and Dale was also interviewed by Osage County investigators the same week.

During a phone conversation which he allowed me to record as usual, Dale told me that the investigators had driven to his home in Arkansas twice and conducted several phone interviews as well. The questions they asked him were similar to the ones they had asked Paul and they indicated to Dale that the Mullendore murder was indeed solved. Unfortunately, Dale died of heart failure not long after this conversation. Will this mystery ever be solved and why has it taken so long? The answers to these questions rest with Osage County District Attorney Rex Duncan, a man with a reputation for seeing justice served.

Till next week I'll see you down the road....

Ghost Ranch and the St. James Hotel

Welcome back. After a few days spent at the Ghost Ranch in north central New Mexico, I've come back to Bartlesville a new man. The magic of place and the experience of walking in the footsteps of the famous people who have stayed there one sees life from a different perspective. The early Indian people who lived in the area and the early Spanish explorers of 1598 called it "El Valle de la Pierra Lumbre" which translates as 'The Valley of the Shining Stone."

In the early 1920s Carol Stanley opened a dude ranch on the property where she hosted many wealthy families and celebrities such as Charles Lindbergh and the great conductor Leopold Stokowski. Editor and publisher Arthur Pack visited the ranch in 1933 and fell in love with it. He eventually purchased Ghost Ranch and over time he acquired additional acreage around it, enlarging the ranch to a total of twenty-one thousand acres. At the same time, artist Georgia O'Keefe began visiting and after a long negotiation she finally bought seven and a half acres from Arthur Pack, just a short distance from his home. O'Keefe built a house on her land which still stands today.

In order to protect Ghost Ranch from development Arthur Pack and his wife donated the entire property to the Presbyterian Church in 1955 to be used as an educational center. Today the ranch can accommodate over 300 guests who are able to enjoy not only the beauty of the multi-colored hills and sandstone cliffs but also the legends surrounding the site. Rumor has it that outlaws from years past buried sacks of gold somewhere in the canyons, amongst many dead bodies. There are also stories about monsters that roam at night but no one who sees them lives to talk. The locals call Ghost Ranch "Rancho de los Brujos" or "Ranch of the Witches" and tell you about six-foot-tall earth babies covered in red hair and ghost cows with wings. Others recall meeting the scientists who developed the atom bomb during World War II in Los Alamos, just a few miles west of the ranch.

It's kind of scary after the sun goes down here when you can hear cries that sound like people in pain. Everything is peaceful during the day when you can hike trails called Chimney Rock and Kitchen Mesa. For real hikers there's the Box Canyon trail where dinosaur fossils are common This is a place where the spirit world and the present-day human world come together and it's about as beautiful as it gets. Just an hour and a half drive northeast of Santa Fe, Ghost Ranch is another American treasure that the Original Buffalo Dale highly recommends. If you want to know more about rates and reservations go to www.ghostranch.org or visit my website www.originalbuffal-odale.com but beware, like me this trip might just rearrange the way you look at life.

Another inspiring place that I've written about before is Philmont Scout Ranch. Just a few miles outside of Cimarron, New Mexico along the old Santa Fe trail, Philmont is not only one of my favorite places but was also one of legendary oil man Waite Phillips' as well. Philmont sits at 6,430 feet above sea level and the first thing you see is the mountains. Majestic to say the least. Your visit there will be filled with history as well.

A tour of the Waite Phillips home is a must along with a visit to the celebrated St. James Hotel where many an early day cowboy met his death. Buffalo Bill, Clay Allen, Jesse James and many others stayed at the St. James and you can too. But beware, ghost sitings are common here. The St. James is owned by Oklahoma businessman and philanthropist Bob Funk and it is as much a museum as a hotel. All the guest rooms in the original part of the building are decorated in old west style from the 1800s. The common areas are filled with western art and artifacts including original Will James drawings, a collection of spurs and paintings of the hotel's famous guests. This is another of my favorite stops whenever I'm traveling in this part of the world and for sure it's a must if you're out that way. As an added bonus, elk, deer, turkey and even bear can be seen in the arca on a regular basis.

I'm out of space now but next week I'll have more from my travels in New Mexico. Till then, I'll see you down the road....

Philbrook and Philmonte

Welcome back. In 1927 Waite Phillips built two beautiful homes, Villa Philbrook and Villa Philmonte both of which were designed by architect Edmond Buehler Delk. In Tulsa Philbrook is located at 2727 South Rockford Road and looks similar to the home Waite and his wife Genevieve built in New Mexico. The exterior of Villa Philbrook is distinguished by fancy wrought iron fencing and the grounds feature stone fountains and reflecting pools set in lush gardens that were laid out by Waite himself. The interior has floors of marble, teak, walnut and oak with elaborate European silk curtains hanging above giant windows. There are stucco ceilings in the library, the study and the music room and on the walls are hand painted murals of dancing maidens.

With Genevieve's direction the main part of Villa Philbrook is European in style but Waite had his man cave on the lower level or basement if you could call it that. A big American Indian art collector, Waite filled the rooms with tribal rugs and mounts of buffalo, elk and mountain lions he had shot. He didn't have to worry about space for his collections because architect Delk had completed his other house, Villa Philmonte in New Mexico soon after.

Designed in a style that was similar to his Tulsa home but without as much square footage, Villa Philmonte had a massive yard. With close to three hundred thousand acres at an elevation of around six thousand five hundred feet above sea level, sitting on his porch looking out at the mountains Waite could see as far up as ten thousand feet to peaks that were covered in snow, some all year around. He told his friends and business associates that there was no place on earth like it and many of them came to visit. Villa Philmonte also reflected Genevieve's interest in European style as well as Waite's love of Native American and western art.

Reading up more on Waite in the Boy Scout library located just a few blocks from the villa I learned that he had been fascinated by the history of this area that had once been part of an enormous land grant from Mexico. He loved to tell houseguests about an old cabin that had been right where the villa was now located and that Kit Carson, Buffalo Bill, Jesse James and a slew of other well-known western characters had actually slept in the area. Will Rogers and Wiley Post were bound to have heard these stories when they stopped over for a visit on their way to Alaska in 1935. Waite took one of the last photos of the two in the gardens at the villa before their tragic deaths a few days later.

Charles Dawes who was Vice President in Calvin Coolidge's administration came to Philmonte regularly as did well known Tulsan Bill Skelly, oil man E.W. Marland and big brother Frank. When he was interviewed by author Michael Wallis for the book Beyond the Hills, the Journey of Waite Phillips, Waite's son Chope recalled that many of the major figures of the time came to visit the family at Villa Philmonte during the seventeen years thcy lived there.

Unfortunately for all of us Chope, Waite and Genevieve are gone now but friends Villa Philmonte is not and that's where I've been staying on and off for the last few months. Not in a cabin or tent but right in the same room Will stayed in. Right where the famous actress Yvonne DeCarlo unpacked her suitcase. The same room where Frank and Jane would have dressed for diner. With the old swimming pool right out my window I can almost hear Waite and Frank talking oil while Jane and Genevieve discuss the latest Paris fashions. Yes, I'm in historic room #4 at the Philmonte mansion in Cimarron, New Mexico and I might just stay for a while.

Here's the local snow report. Central New Mexico continues to be dry and the lack of precipitation is making it rough on the ski areas. As for wildlife sighting, I can see elk, deer and turkey right outside my window. No bear but lots of buffalo on Ted Turner's big ranch which is just five or six miles away.

Till next time I'll see ya down the road……

Waite Philips' Legacy

Welcome back. Once again, I'm taking you back in time this week to January 27, 1964 when Lyndon B. Johnson was President; the Beatles had a hit song in the U.S. with I Want to Hold Your Hand, Ian Fleming's On Her Majesty's Secret Service was a bestselling book and it was also the last day in the life of a great philanthropist. You might say it all started a few days earlier when Waite Phillips sent his son Chope to check out the Philmont Scout Ranch for him. By then Waite had already given the Boy Scout organization well over one hundred thousand acres of land. He had also established an endowment to support the upkeep of the ranch and any needed building projects.

Waite's birthday was coming up on January 19th and at 81 he wanted to be assured that the Boy Scout Ranch would be secure in the future. During the preceding few months his health had been deteriorating and after suffering a couple of heart attacks he had a nurse on call twenty-four hours a day. In his book Beyond the Hills: The Journey of Waite Phillips author Michael Wallis describes Waite's last four months on earth. According to Wallace, Waite enjoyed remembering his youth and the days of making millions with his brothers Frank and L.E. As most people around here know, the Phillips brothers came from Iowa and went on to establish one of the biggest independent oil companies in the world. Waite eventually split off from his brothers and formed his own successful company. When he eventually sold that company, he became one of the richest men in the country.

In 1964 all that was years in the past for Waite but his love for the scout ranch that was now named Philmont was on his mind. He had already laid out his will giving thousands of dollars to his grandchildren and other relatives. He'd also left money to his staff and several friends. The University of Southern California would receive a three-million-dollar gift and another seven million would go to other colleges and charities.
Among several hospitals Bartlesville's Jane Phillips Hospital

received $200,000. Waite's wife would be left millions in property, along with personal possessions and cash. He also provided additional salary for his long-term employees.

As January 27th approached Waite knew everything was in order and after receiving a good report from his son Chope who had just returned from a four day stay at Philmont, he felt happy and rejuvenated enough to take a walk. At 1:30 AM on January 27th, the farm boy from Iowa who had built an empire in both oil and real estate and then given most of his wealth away, died.

I've written about this great man in the past and honoring the anniversary of his death only seems right. If you get a chance to read it, the local library has Wallis' book Beyond the Hills or even better take a trip like me to Waite's favorite place in the world, Philmont. It is open all year round for tours but I warn you that at sixty-five hundred feet it can be quite cold in the winter.

Till next time, from sixty-five hundred feet I'll see ya down the road...............

THE LETTERS

FROM DAMON 'CHUB' ANDERSON

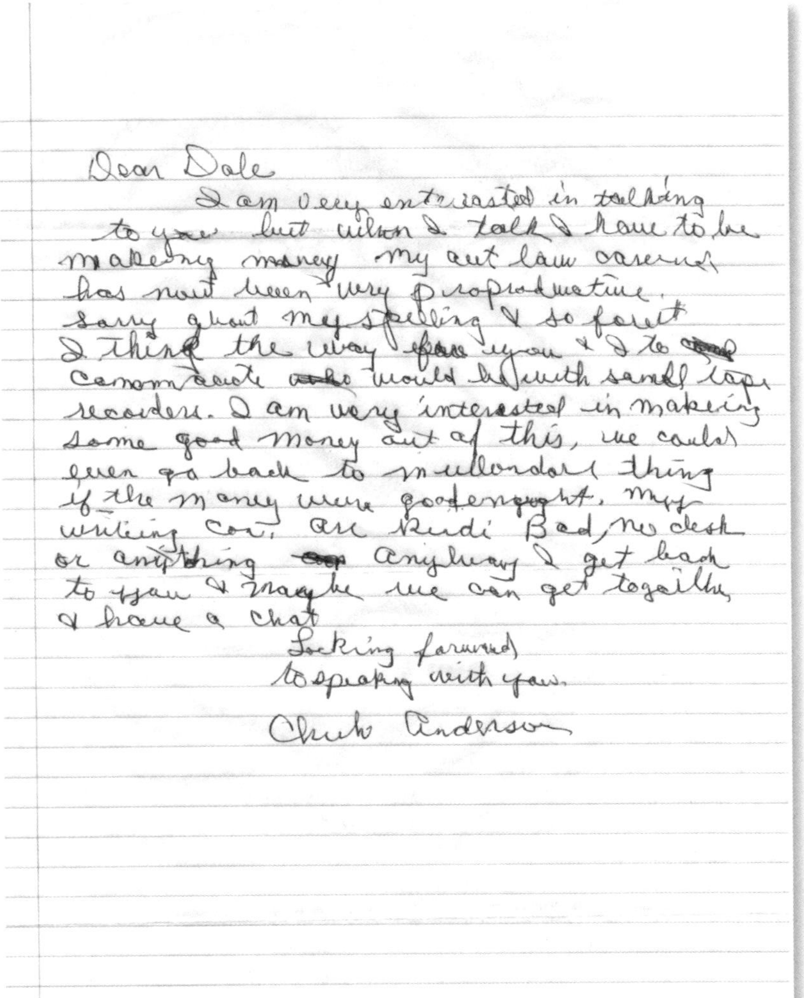

Dear Dale

I am very intereasted in talking to you but when I talk I have to be makeing money my out law careers has not been very proprodmative. sorry about my spelling & so forth I think the way you & I to comunicate would be with small tape recorders. I am very interested in makeing some good money out of this, we could even go back to mullondarl thing if the money were good enought. my writing con. are kindi Bad, no desk or anything anyway I get back to you & maybe we can get togather & have a chat

Looking forward
to speaking with you.

Chuck Anderson

Dear Dale

I hope you make it up this weekend
I look fareward to ~~talking~~ with you
if you will call Lonnie tell him
not to ~~see~~ send and money to that
Samuel Jones he turned out to be a
crook like most Blacks are I went
a head & wrote so if you don't come
this weekend my letter would get
there

~~I~~ See you this weekend
Damon

Dear Dale
I haven't heard from you in
over a wek thought I'would drop you
a few lines I heard from Bill Kurtis
Sectary he was wanting a
Interview the preson wasn't alowe
a lowe that he & she would have to
get a Vistor pass. I didn't like
it to well when in sedan he come out
& Ask me what I thought that Gary
Glanz thought I was the one who
killed E.S. you could line up 100 people
& probaly 50 of them would say
that, Anyway when he wanted
to talk to me about more book deals
I wrote & tall him if he had so
much faith in Glanz go talk
talk to him, I haven't heard from
them since he thinks he has the
market cornered on who I talk to
I let him know that wasn't the deal
Any way I'll wait to here from you
Dale if you well send the Guy 50.00
if will Get to me I'll explain later
I'm going to go with you on any book
or any other publicity deal the Gary
adress is over

Dear Dale

It's your old buddy hey
dale I might be a little short
have Lonnie or somebody send
me a couple hundred if you will
Michelle martin wanting to
send me some money but I
didn't want to be beholding
to them any ways I'll talk to
you next weekend

The old outlaw
Damon Anderson

Mr. Lewis

Chub here, I hope you didn't send that rat Bosch any thing I had a good friend write because my hands were so stiff. I hope we can get togeather eye to eye be fore long. I kinda wrote Mr Kurtis off because of the Gary Glanz deal Gary was a privite investergater for Linda's lawer he tryed to trip me up once & I never forgot it he had ~~I~~ a thunderbird ford ~~and~~ all recordings with bugs & ~~try~~ tryed to go me to admit ~~sh~~ ~~scratching~~ shooting E.C. tay telling me wat a hero I would be E.C. was one of my better friends at the time Glanz alway thought he was the only one in the game with any Brains. I think he had the hots for Linda. any way thats anothr story. my if our 1st Book does good we can finish the 1st one.

In your last letter you ~~mention~~ wrote something a bout Todd Anderson please tell me what that was about

well Lewis Im going to close for now write soon

Damon Anderson

Death threat from someone in Montana after my visit there.

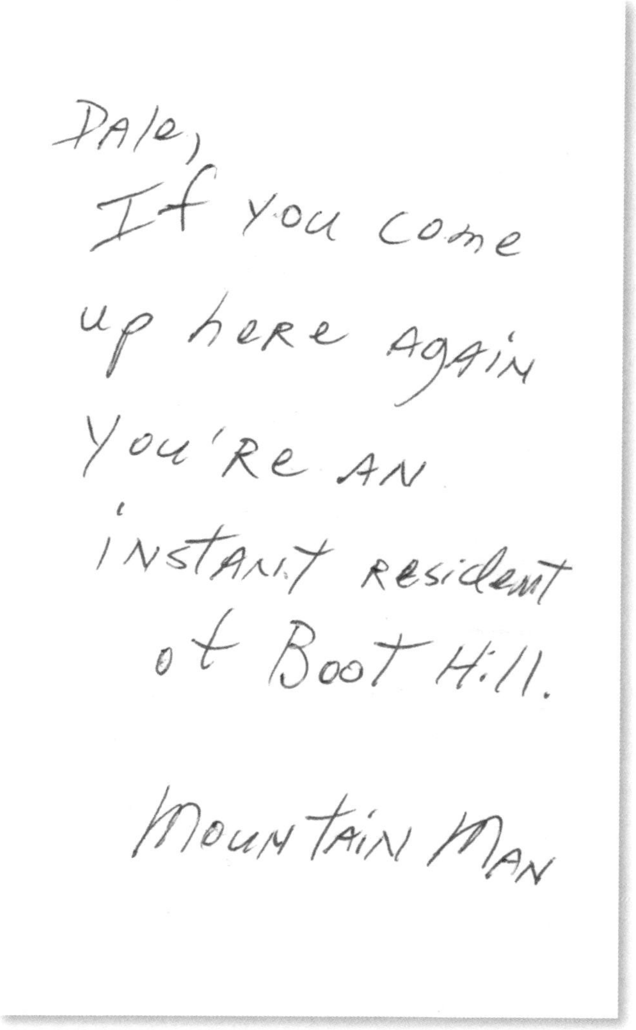
Dale,
If you come
up here again
you're an
instant resident
of Boot Hill.

Mountain Man

THE LETTERS

FROM KATSY WHITTENBURG

Damon Lehult Anderson # 86529
Lansing Correctional Facility
Lansing, Kansas 66043

Dear Lehult

So many years have gone by and I feel such a strong need to come talk with you. I am sorry you are not well.

Several people have told me that you are willing to see me. I appreciate that and if you would put me on your visitation list I will come immediately.

I understand that it is necessary to fill out forms before I would be allowed to see you. If you are agreeable please do what you can to send these forms to me.

Hoping to hear from you soon and see you as soon as possible.

Sincerely
Katsy

Katsy Whittenburg
620 S. Taylor
Amarillo, Texas
79101

Dear Tehub ~

Thank you so much for your nice letter ~ I have sent my visitation form back and waiting to hear from them on when I can come –

Tehub it will be 36 years in September that you have lived with this heart ache and knowledge ~

I loved E.C. more than words can express. E.C. was a wonderful brother and always watched over me. He was a good, kind, loyal, fun loving father, friend, brother and son. I have always felt so helpless over his death.

Tehub, I always liked you and felt you and E.C. had a good relationship – and I know how much he had trusted you in the past. A lot of trust was placed in you by my whole family.

Tehub I just want to know the truth of why and how E.C. was killed. I feel you

have suffered enough by living
with your knowledge of that
nite — And I feel empty by
not knowing what really
happened — the hurt - the
grief - the helplessness of 36 years
is alot ~

I trust in you and
admire your silence - to me -
only you and I ever have to
know the truth.

I am looking for the book
for you and I will get you one
and send it right to you.

Again, thank you, for agreeing
to see me - I think it will be
good for us both ~ If there is
anything I am allowed to send
or bring to you at any time
please let me know ~

Your friend,
Katsy

P.S.
Your writting was great —

Hi Tekul
I have talked with Dale Lewis
several times. He seems to be very
interested in you and what you
have to say. I support your
project together. I feel he will
be honest with you.
Tekul it was good to visit
with you, many of your answers
and stories made me laugh and
some made me cry inside. I really
have only had two questions ever—
WHY and WHO
People have been so quick to try
and sensationalize a story about a
family they know nothing about, that
I never wanted to hear their stories.
You are the only one I know that
could answer those two questions.
So if you can find it in your
heart Tekul, would you write down
for me or at least give me your
opinion of why this happened, an
accurate accounting of the evening,
who was at the ranch that nite,
why was murder necessary, why
you felt it necessary to protect
someone who had just murdered

2

your friend. Surely this knowledge has been difficult and caused you hurt and pain. Just knowing you were considered a "trusted" friend. You were depended on by a friend, a friend who needed protecting, at a time when he needed support. Why do you feel it necessary to protect someone who had done this horrible thing. A lot of trust was placed in you – and I trust you to make the right decision on behalf of E.L. This is the only way you have to make that peace with your self and the rest of us, by setting straight all you know about that evening.

I have written and thrown away so many letters to you – not knowing how to say what was on my mind – I do want you to know how much it has meant to me that you allowed ~~me~~ me to come visit with you –

Thank you
Katsy

January 2, 2007

BEFORE THE DEW

THE OBITUARYS

James Andrew "Jimmie" Whittenburg, III

January 14, 1933 – December 6, 2016

James Andrew "Jimmie" Whittenburg, III – rancher, banker, cattle raiser, oil & gas entrepreneur, aviator and Special Texas Ranger – died peacefully at his home in Dallas, TX. He was 83 years old.

Jimmie was born on January 14, 1933 in Amarillo, TX, the second of three children, and only son, to James Andrew Whittenburg, Jr. and Catharine Coble Whittenburg. His parents were both from prominent pioneer ranching families who had started in the Texas Panhandle around the time of the Civil War. He attended Bivins Elementary school, Elizabeth Nixon Junior High School and Amarillo High School, but obtained the majority of his education by actively operating his family's ranches in the Texas Panhandle and New Mexico. "All of my interests were on the ranch, not in the classroom," as he liked to say. He later completed courses in geology at Amarillo College, as well as law enforcement training at the Panhandle Regional Law Enforcement Academy.

Jimmie met Kathryn Jeanne Price of Stratford, TX in the spring of 1951. They were married on December 7, 1952 in Portales, NM. They honeymooned in Acapulco, attended bullfights in Mexico City, and settled back in Amarillo, where together they began to build and raise their family: Jeanne Price was born on August 25, 1953; Lelah Elizabeth "Liz" was born on October 24, 1954; James Andrew "Jim or Jimbo" was born on October 21, 1955; Catharine Coble "C.C." was born on December 15, 1956 and Leslie Sommer on April 3, 1965. Jimmie loved being a dedicated father and parenting the children with Jeanne. He was a role model, and unparalleled inspiration to all of those, young and old, who came in contact with him throughout his life.

He and Jeanne enjoyed 42 years of marriage until she tragically died in 1995, when a helicopter that Jimmie was piloting encountered severe turbulence and crashed. He was gravely injured but survived. Despite overwhelming physical injuries and emotional loss of his wife, his indomitable spirit, grit and surmounting perseverance spurred his recovery from the catastrophic accident. None of this could have transpired without the love support of his family, who Jimmie credited with saving his life.

In the summer of 1999, he met with Katsy Mullendore of the Cross Bell Ranch in Oklahoma. They were married on September 14, 2002 at his Sapello Ranch in New Mexico. Jimmie said, "I've had fortune beyond odds that anybody could hope for, and it happened not once but twice in a lifetime . . . what were the odds of meeting a woman I could love after having the most special person in my life at my side?" Katsy continued to be a resplendent, gracious and unwavering companion.

Jimmie showed an early enthusiasm for aviation, and learned to fly airplanes at the age of 17, purchasing his first airplane, a Beechcraft V-Rail Bonanza, in 1950; he continued to be involved in leasing and flying of various aircrafts for all his life. He also became a licensed helicopter pilot, which saved time in his travel between Amarillo and the ranches. Work and personal adventure to all the corners of the globe instigated Jimmie's piloting of single-engines, turboprops, piston-powered planes and business jets. "I believed that to do more, all I needed was to get up earlier and have a faster airplane." His aircraft included Tradewind Turbines, Cessna and Beechcraft dealerships and ownership of an Airport in Amarillo.

The one consistent title on Jimmie's highly diversified résumé that he liked most was that of a rancher. His lineage of homesteaders, cattle ranchers, traders, buffalo hunters and frontiersmen was generations deep. He learned the ranching and cattle business from his father, mother and grandparents at the Turkey Track Ranch in the Texas Panhandle. He later owned and operated ranches in the Panhandle and New Mexico. From the mid-1950s he not only was dealing in ranching, oil and gas, aviation and investments through farming, feedlots, raising cattle, real estate, banking, insurance, and a hotel venture.

His marked leadership ability and fair, honest dealing were well known in his many business dealings. He was director, president and CEO of the First Bank of Stratford from 1960-1986. Helped found Stratford of Texas, Inc., which in 1972 became the largest cattle feeding company in the United States and was president of the Texas & Southwestern Cattle Raiser's Association (TSCRA) from 1975-1977.

From the 1970s through the early 2000s, he was a director of the American National Bank, Fort Worth National Bank Holding Company, Mid-Continent Life Insurance Company, National Cowboy Hall of Fame & Western Heritage Center, National Cattlemen's Association, New Mexico Cattle Growers Association, Oklahoma Cattlemen's Association, National Finance Credit Corporation / Texas Livestock Marketing Association, Panhandle Plains Historical Society, Special Texas Rangers Commission, Texas Cattle Feeder's Association, Missouri Beef Packers (later MBPXL), Texas Organized Crime Prevention Council, appointed commissioner of the Texas Alcoholic Beverage Commission and was an organizing member of the Texas Land & Mineral Owners Association (TMLA). In the 1970s and early 80s, he served on the boards of MD Anderson Cancer Center, Texas' War on Drugs Committee, St. Anthony's Hospital and Amarillo Globe-News.

Jimmie was appointed to the position of Special Texas Ranger and served from 1961-1974. He was then a member of the Former Texas Ranger's Association from 1973-1978, and Executive Committee member of the Texas Rangers Commemorative Commission and Hall of Fame.

He was preceded in death by his wife, Jeanne Price Whittenburg, his son James Andrew "Jim or Jimbo" Whittenburg IV, and by his sister, Catharine Coble Whittenburg McAnnally.

He will be forever by those who knew him, especially his surviving relatives are: his wife, Katsy Whittenburg of Dallas; his four daughters and their husbands Jeanne Latimer (Bob), Liz Redwine (Ras V), C.C. Armstrong (Stewart) and Leslie el-Effendi (Wicky); his sister Fancie Whittenburg; his fourteen grandchildren Catharine Whittenburg Vexler, James Andrew "J." Whittenburg V, Price Latimer, Ras Redwine VI, Robert Weber "Roby" Latimer Jr., Coble Armstrong Jorgensen, Elizabeth Redwine Brenner, Stewart Larkin Armstrong, Mia Armstrong Brous, Sarah Latimer Hager, Alexandra Latimer Baldwin, Adham Hisssam el-Effendi, Leslie Forrest el-Effendi and Elizabeth "Elli" Jeanne el-Effendi; be his step-children, numerous cousins, nieces, nephews, and soon-to-be fourteen great-grandchildren.

BEFORE THE DEW

Katsy Mullendore Whittenburg

Katsy Mullendore Whittenburg went to be with her Lord and Savior on February 21, 2017, at her home in Dallas. Katsy was born on March 7, 1940, in Tulsa, Oklahoma, to Kathleen and Eugene C. Mullendore. She was proud of her cattle ranching and American Indian heritage. Her grandfather, Eer C. Mullendore made the Cherokee Strip Land Run in Oklahoma in 1893. Her great grandfather Charlie Brown was Osage Chief Shon-kah. She was raised on the Cross Bell Ranch in Northeastern Oklahoma where she developed a love for horses, cattle, and a pet buffalo, Geronimo, that she broke to ride. She attended elementary school in a one room school house built on the ranch to educate the children of the people who lived and worked there. She later attended Gulfpark Boarding School in Gulfport, Mississippi. She attended the University of Oklahoma and the University of Texas where she was a member of the Pi Beta Phi Sorority, Katsy married John W. Mecom, Jr. in 1961. They had four children and she was a loving and dedicated mother. Her kind and giving spirit called her to serve selflessly and volunteer her time to a multitude or organizations in Houston for the next thirty years. She also served on thc Osage Nation Foundation Board, the Woolaroc Museum Trustee Board, and fund raised extensively for Eldercare in Bartlesville, Oklahoma. In the summer of 1999 Katsy met the love of her life, James Andrew "Jimmie" Whittenburg III. They were married

September 14, 2002 at Jimmie's Sapello Ranch in New Mexico. Together they blended their large and diverse families. They enjoyed traveling around the world and spending time at their ranches and home in Pebble Beach, California. Katsy will be forever remembered in the hearts of those who loved her. Her grace and unwavering kindness touched the lives of countless people as she was considered a friend by many. She was the epitome of a lady. She loved life and lived it well. As she neared the end, she smiled and said, "We had a pretty good ride, didn't we?" She was preceeded in death by her beloved husband, James Andrew "Jimmie" Whittenburg (January 14, 1933, December 6, 2016). She is survived by her son John W. Mecom 3 and wife Emily, daughter Katsy M. Cluck and husband Monte, daughter Mary Elizabeth M. Hahnfeld and daughter Kethleen M. Fogarty, and her twelve grandchildren Hanna Elizabeth Mecom, Merritt Jay Mecom, Lilah Ellen Mecom, Wyatt Whitfield Mecom, Kaysha Cluck Sparling, Kallie Cluck Hauschild, Monte Dean Cluck II, Madeline Elizabeth Hahnfeld, Kathleen Alexis Fogarty, Abigail Meccom Fogarty, Danny Coe Fogarty, Luke Mecom Fogarty, and her step children and great granchildren. Private services will he held at the family ranch cemetery in Copan, Oklahoma. In lieu of flowers, Katsy's family requests that donations be considered to the charity or your choice or to Washington County Elder Care, 1223 Swan Drive, Bartlesville, OK 74006 or to the VNA of Dallas, 1600 Viceroy Drive, Suite 400, Dallas, TX 75235.

SPECIAL THANKS

Steve Adams
Mike & Diane Diamond
The late Charlie Harris
Mike Kelly
Elise Kilpatrick & Gary Kuch
John Nickel
Jerry Stover
Deirdre McArdle
Bob Funk
Gentner Drummond
Harvey Grauberger
Rhonda Yocham – Yocham's Custom Leather Saddlery
Nolan Jones
Keith Aitken
The Bartlesville Examiner Enterprise
The Tulsa World
Brace Books – Ponca City, OK
Best of Books – Edmond, OK
Jude's Health & Java House

A special thanks to all my readers

And as always I want to thank my daughter
Loretta Eleanor Bartlett Lewis who is still
the inspiration for everything I do.